Digitally Dysfunctional

An analog description of our digital dystopia

TABLE OF CONTENTS

Prologue:
Welcome to the Age of Cellular Lunacy

Greetings, brave analog soul.

If you're reading this, congratulations: you've either picked up this book intentionally (which already makes you smarter than 87% of the population), or you've accidentally stumbled onto it while searching for a phone charger in a bookstore that sells more coffee than literature. Either way, welcome. And buckle up — it's going to be a deeply uncomfortable ride through the manicured landfill we now call modern society.

This is not a memoir. This is not a call to action. This is not even a guidebook. This is a **sarcastic scream into the pixelated abyss**, a therapeutic roast session for anyone who's ever wanted to throw someone's phone under a bus — preferably while they were using it to record a video of that same bus.

The Glorious Downfall of Common Sense

Once upon a time — say, 1994 — people used phones to *call* people. Crazy, I know. You pressed buttons, heard a dial tone, and waited. You couldn't stream your lunch, swipe through strangers, or ruin your cousin's wedding by Face Timing your dog. And somehow, miraculously, we survived.

But now? We live in a world where a human being will sprint into oncoming traffic for a selfie with a squirrel. Where friendships are measured in likes. Where toddlers know how to unlock a tablet before they can spell their own name. Welcome to the **Digital Dystopia**, where everyone's online, no one's present, and your grandmother just accidentally live-streamed her nostrils for 18 minutes.

This Book Exists Because People Like You Are Tired

You, the reader, are likely part of a shrinking tribe. You remember *conversations* — those weird vocal exchanges people used to have before every dialogue was reduced to emojis and cryptic abbreviations that now require urban dictionary translation. (Yes, "💀" means "I'm laughing." No, you're not dying. Yet.)

You're probably exhausted. Exhausted from listening to strangers' phone calls in cafés, watching couples ignore each other at dinner while curating #relationshipgoals, and navigating sidewalks where every third person is moving like a drunk zombie, eyes locked on a 6.5-inch screen of dopamine drizzle.

You're tired of people narrating their own lives in public, on speakerphone, with all the subtlety of a foghorn in a funeral. You're tired of pretending not to hear someone's entire medical history because "privacy" now only applies to browser settings.

So here we are.

What This Book Will *Not* Do

Let's manage your expectations.

This book will not fix the problem. Oh no. That ship sailed when humanity decided that clout was currency and TikTok dances qualified as skill sets. We're way past salvation. We now worship at the altar of Wi-Fi, sacrifice our attention spans to algorithms, and treat airplane mode like a near-death experience.

This book will not offer helpful digital detox tips like "go outside" or "try a yoga retreat." You've read those before. You rolled your eyes then, and you'll roll your eyes again now. Plus, going outside requires pants. Let's not kid ourselves.

This book will not politely ask for better behavior. We tried that already. Remember those adorable "quiet car" signs on trains? Yeah. Neither does anyone else.

What This Book *Will* Do

It will **shame**, **mock**, and **relentlessly roast** the ever-growing cesspool that is modern phone culture.

- We'll skewer the **public phone talkers**, the volume-immune vuvuzelas who think every subway ride needs a bonus podcast episode.

- We'll dissect the **FaceTimers in grocery stores**, the cinematic auteurs who film their entire fruit aisle journey like it's a high-budget sequel to *Bananas: The Reckoning*.

- We'll honor the **headphone-averse sociopaths**, who treat shared spaces as their personal audition for The Loudest Human Alive.

We will pay tribute to the martyrs — the analog angels — who still know how to sit quietly, read a book, or gaze out a window *without filming it for their Instagram story*. Saints, all of them. Probably hiding in plain sight. Or extinct. Hard to tell anymore.

A Celebration of the Analog

But don't worry — we're not all doom and gloom. This book is also a love letter to the lost arts. The delicate beauty of **conversation, quiet,** and **not filming everything like you're the director of a documentary no one asked for.**

We celebrate the sacred act of *being bored* — a concept now classified as a mental health emergency. We tip our hats to eye contact, handwritten notes, and listening without a podcast narrator voice.

You may weep, you may rage, you may laugh until your spine cracks — all appropriate responses. Because this isn't just a book. It's a mirror. A very shiny, brutally honest, fingerprint-smeared mirror held up to a society that thought giving everyone a smartphone would lead to global enlightenment.

Oops.

A Word of Warning

If you are one of the offenders — if you are reading this while FaceTiming someone about your foot cream in the middle of a crowded bus — put the book down. Gently. Step away. Reflect. Consider therapy. Or at the very least, consider *headphones*. This book may not be for you. Unless, of course, you enjoy the sting of well-earned sarcasm. In which case, welcome aboard, you magnificent trainwreck of a person. You're exactly the type we need to reach.

One Final Thought Before We Begin

We are not anti-technology. No, no. We're just anti-**idiotic use of technology**. There's a difference.

This isn't about going off-grid, churning butter, and weaving your own socks (though if that's your thing, respect). This is about demanding **basic, functioning human decency** in a world obsessed with engagement, followers, and filming every waking moment like it's *The Truman Show: Narcissism Edition.*

This is your guidebook. Your survival manual. Your emotional support rant.

It's the book you read while muttering "Yes, EXACTLY!" under your breath on a crowded train as someone next to you watches conspiracy videos at full blast.

It's the book you gift your cousin who Snapchatted a funeral.

It's the book you toss at someone's feet like an analogue intervention disguised as humor.

And if we've done our job — by the time you're done reading — you'll laugh, wince, and maybe even rethink the next time you reach for your phone in a shared space.

Or not. We're not hopeful. But damn, we're sarcastic.

Welcome to *Digitally Dysfunctional*. May your battery die when you need it most.

Chapter 1
Commuting Woes
The psychological gamble that is our daily sojourn.

Welcome to the daily cattle drive of the modern soul—where humanity packs itself into metal tubes on wheels and pretends not to exist. It's crowded. It's loud. It smells vaguely of stress, fast food, and someone's forgotten gym bag. And everyone, everyone, is plugged in and tuned out. Earbuds in. Or not. Empathy off. This isn't public transportation—it's an emotional vacuum seal with BO and Bluetooth. Prepare yourself, dear reader, for a journey through the groaning bowels of mass transit, where phone screens glow brighter than hope and self-awareness is as extinct as punctual trains.

Bus-ted – Welcome to the Screaming Steel Sauna of Social Despair

Ah yes, the city bus—a sacred space once reserved for the occasional nod to a fellow human, the calming hum of a sputtering diesel engine, and the soothing squeak of vinyl seats aged to a crackling crisp. In the golden, long-forgotten era before smartphones, it was a humble habitat of heads-down, eyes-forward silence—a momentary meditation station on wheels. And now? Now it's a mobile madhouse, a four-wheeled freakshow barreling through pothole-ridden streets, brimming with belligerent buffoons and Bluetooth-blaring baboons.

Let us begin this journey into Purgatory on pavement by first boarding the morning bus. You remember mornings, right? That mythical time before sunrise when coffee and hope briefly coexisted. But hope, dear reader, it is now a casualty of the 7:18 a.m. Bus of Broken Boundaries. As you step aboard—dodging wet footprints, sticky seats, and the scent of someone's eau de yesterday's regrets—you're immediately greeted by the dulcet tones of someone's full-volume FaceTime call. A conversation not about anything urgent, mind you, but an animated debate over whether Taylor Swift's newest ex deserves public sympathy or social execution. Spoiler: he doesn't. Neither does your eardrum.

Across from you sits *the Tinny Terrorist*—one earbud dangling unused like a limp ramen noodle while their phone bleats out TikTok's at a volume that rivals a smoke alarm. Every other video is a looping audio clip of someone lip-syncing with the kind of misplaced confidence you usually only see in karaoke bars or padded rooms. The volume? Obnoxiously overcompensating.

The speaker? A tiny, trembling traitor to bass and clarity alike. It's less "entertainment" and more "audio assault."

And there, by the window, sits **the Candy Crusher,** elbows flailing like an orchestra conductor with palsy, annihilating digital jellybeans with a fervor typically reserved for riot police. Every "ping!" and "pop!" is another stab to your sanity, a tiny electronic dagger to the eardrum delivered by someone who believes their seat fee includes auditory domination of the entire vehicle. Their faces are a slack-jawed mural of concentration; their brow furrowed like a wrinkled road map to mediocrity.

And in the center of this digital circus: you. You, noble relic of a forgotten era, clutching your book—or worse, your own silenced phone—like a chastity belt against the orgy of obnoxiousness around you. You stare blankly ahead, trying not to make eye contact with the dude two seats away watching a UFC knockout compilation while chewing gum with the grace of a goat eating gravel.

Headphones? An endangered species. Mute buttons? Mythical creatures. Volume control? A long-forgotten legend lost to the sands of time. Every trip is a sensory slap, a screeching testament to the digital delusion that every moment must be documented, broadcast, or turned into a 10-second dopamine hit for five whole followers.

The Cellphone Senator, who insists on holding their phone like a walkie-talkie and narrating every second of their existence. They shout into their device as if they're phoning Jupiter, blissfully unaware—or worse, blissfully indifferent—to the cacophonous chaos they're inflicting on every ear.

Their conversation topics range from hilariously mundane ("I told her I *don't* like pickles") to horrifyingly intimate ("And then my rash got worse"), each sentence a verbal ambush no commuter consented to.

And then, the ultimate auditory insult: ***the Portable DJ***. This peculiar primate believes that the back of the bus is their personal dance floor. Armed with a Bluetooth speaker and a playlist of bass-boosted abominations, they proceed to host an unsolicited EDM rave during rush hour.

Steel Cage Confessional – The Streetcar Standoff of Screeching Screens

The streetcar. That quaint, clangy compromise between modern convenience and a Victorian torture device. A rolling iron coffin gliding gracefully through the city at the speed of a hung over tortoise. If the bus is hell's waiting room, then the streetcar is the flaming corridor leading directly to it, adorned with cracked windows, mysterious seat stains, and the soul-shattering chorus of incoming notifications from every electronic idiot on board.

Attempting to move your way down the car, there's the ***Clump of Doom.*** A stationary mob of digital narcissists who've collectively decided that moving to the back of the streetcar would violate their sacred Wi-Fi signal. Like bloated barnacles on a rusting ship, they anchor themselves mid-car with earbuds loosely dangling like limp spaghetti and screens aglow with Candy Crush, as though those high scores will one day feed their families.

Just when your inner peace seems beyond salvage, in struts the ***Selfie Savant.*** This narcissistic nomad, equipped with a collapsible ring light and the swagger of a runway model in a windstorm, stakes out a corner by the window smeared with fingerprints and unidentifiable goo. They strike pose after pouty pose, tilting their head like a confused flamingo, capturing a hundred shots of their own navel as if the Mona Lisa herself resided within.

Lurking nearby, the **Cellphone Senator** launches into a monologue that would make a Shakespearean soliloquy sound subtle. You don't just overhear their conversation—you live it. You feel *Debbie's betrayal*. You endure the *rash update*. You mourn the *missed Costco run*. Each syllable spat with such volume and conviction, one would think they were testifying before Congress.

Next to them sits *the Video Voyeur.* This dull-eyed dunderhead is blissfully unaware of volume buttons as they stream ten-minute clips of people slipping on banana peels or pranksters popping out of garbage bins like traumatized raccoons.

And then, the gods mock us further: a full elementary school field trip board. Picture it—a tidal wave of tiny tyrants, high on freedom and Fruit Roll-Ups, flooding the vehicle like gremlins post-midnight snack. Each child clutches a phone larger than their torso, using it to FaceTime their hamster, blast memes at sonic-boom volume, or record a "vlog" about the incredible experience of sitting. One especially animated angel insists on narrating every passing tree while standing on your foot. The teachers? Dazed hostages, gripping their coffee cups like flotation devices on a sinking ship.

And at this point, you are spiritually bankrupt. You've aged three decades. You've developed new allergies—specifically to humanity. And yet, there's no end in sight.

Subway Suffering – The Cavernous Catacombs of Cell Phone Misery

The subway. The great underground sanctuary where personal space goes to die, and humanity's collective ignorance rises to new, monumental heights. It's not just a mode of transport, dear reader; it's a test of endurance, a gauntlet where your patience will be stretched thinner than the hygiene standards of the average commuter. The subway isn't just about getting from point A to point B; no, it's about seeing how many levels of disrespect, inconsideration, and sheer stupidity humans can achieve in a confined, stinky metal tube before anyone on board spontaneously combust from the sheer idiocy of it all.

The Selfie Savant. This individual, in case you've been blessed enough to avoid them, has taken it upon themselves to document their every move in the most obnoxious way possible. They'll stand directly in front of you, phone in hand, like some sort of performative messiah, attempting to get the perfect angle as if they were the next great model on the cover of "Subway Vogue." God forbid they ever take notice of the hundred-plus people squeezed around them who are all just trying to survive their ride. They move their camera with the delicacy of a drunk toddler and the grace of a giraffe on roller skates. Meanwhile, the poor bastard next to them just wants to get to work without having a picture of his nose taken from five inches away.

The Cellphone Senator. They seem to be everywhere. Like ants at a picnic. That individual who, despite sitting inches from a stranger's face, feels the need to carry on their phone conversation like they're calling the entire population of the subway car into a mandatory town hall meeting. They have no volume control, no sense of appropriateness, and absolutely no shame. You'll be forced to endure their "casual" conversation with Aunt Carol about the latest family drama—whether you want to or not. Aunt Carol's new dog is apparently a very *big deal*. And *God* help you if they're discussing a breakup or arguing about which pizza toppings are acceptable at 8 AM. Your thoughts? Completely irrelevant. The conversation will go on, unimpeded by the disgusted, wide-eyed stares of everyone within a 20-foot radius.

The Gaming Guru's — nature's gift to public spaces. Who *needs* peace and quiet when you can enjoy the 8-bit symphony of laser zaps, dying grunts, and victory jingles echoing through a steel tube at 7:45 a.m.? Nothing says "functioning society" like watching a grown adult scream at Candy Crush like it's the Battle of Helm's Deep. And heaven forbid they lose — now you're treated to a bonus tantrum complete with slapping sounds, deep sighs, and the occasional "THIS GAME IS RIGGED!" Sir, your life is rigged. Invest in headphones. Or a muzzle. Either would be acceptable.

At this point, my good reader, you've lost all hope. You've passed through the collective hellscape that is the subway, your brain fried by digital incompetence, your ears deafened by the cacophony of self-obsessed narcissism. Finally, let's wrap up the experience with the Digital Overload. The individual who has clearly been gifted with the inability to exist in public spaces without their phone permanently fused to their palm. They'll swipe through their apps, oblivious to the world around them, lost in an endless scroll of meaningless content. It's not just a quick check—they're going to watch every video on TikTok, every story on Instagram, and maybe even answer a few emails. They're trapped in their digital echo chamber, a ghost wandering through the subway with non-existent headphones, while the rest of us are left to pray for the sweet release of the next station

The Long-Haul Hell – "Quiet Car" Chaos

The long-haul commuter. The martyr of modern travel. Every day, they ascend from their suburban sanctuaries, making their pilgrimage to the city with all the optimism of someone walking into a lion's den.

You board the train. The train that will whisk you away to a life of delightful anonymity and torturous small talk. The train that promises the precious freedom of an hour or two of personal space—until, of course, that one person who just *has* to invade the designated Quiet Car strolls through. The Quiet Car, that sacred refuge where you're supposed to be left alone with your thoughts, your book, or your half-hearted attempts at pretending you don't hate your job. But no. This, like all good things in life, is fleeting.

Because here comes **the Cellphone Senator**. The person who couldn't grasp the concept of "quiet" if it was spelled out in 48-point font with accompanying interpretive dance. I did say they were everywhere.

They stomp through the car like they're in an audition for a reality TV show. You can't believe your eyes, and then—*the phone comes out*. And it's not just a normal, "quick check-in" phone use. Oh, no. This is a full-on, 30-minute FaceTime session in the middle of the Quiet Car. You try to ignore them, but the volume of their conversation escalates like they're preparing to announce the end of the world on national television. They're recounting every mundane detail of their life with *such conviction*, as though you, the victim, really need to know about their oatmeal or how they spilled coffee on their shoes this morning.

The Long-Haul Texter — the digital woodpecker of the commuter train. Somehow, in the Year of Our Lord 2025, this champion of social cluelessness hasn't discovered the mute button. Instead, we're all treated to the relentless *tick tick tick tick tick* of their touchscreen tap-dancing recital, followed by the soothing *bzzz bzzz bzzz* of incoming gossip. It's like Morse code for the emotionally unavailable. Every tap, a reminder that common courtesy was discontinued in the last software update. And just when you think it's over? *Tick tick tick tick tick* — they're back. Probably typing "omg" for the 19th time. We know. We heard it. So did the next three cars.

 You thought you were lucky to have snagged a seat, now you're sitting beside a **Gaming Guru** grown man who plays a video game where he builds his own farm on his phone. Headphones you might assume? Aren't you adorable.

Ah, behold **Grandma Gloria**, the semi-retired FaceTime DJ of Car 4, gracing us all with her biweekly, full-volume broadcasts of *Little Timmy's mucus production* and *Sophie's interpretive* *screaming.* Gloria, bless her Bluetooth-less heart, holds her phone at full arm's length like a geriatric Spielberg, shouting "CAN YOU SEE ME, SWEETHEART?" And the best part? *She's not wearing headphones.* Because why keep the joy of tiny gremlin giggles to herself when she can share them with 92 unwilling strangers and one crying businessman in the corner?

It doesn't end there, dear commuter. *Oh no.* Not by a long shot. After the initial, desperate wave of digital disasters, the train inevitably starts to fill up. You begin to feel the stirrings of panic as you notice a growing number of disheveled, over-caffeinated, and utterly self-absorbed individuals meandering through the aisles. Cell phones or, no, no it can't be, **laptops** in hand.

The Twice-Daily Trial – Commuting, a Necessary Hell

The twice-a-day *requirement* to endure the cellphone circus that is modern commuting. We do it because we *must*. Not because we want to, not out of some misguided sense of joy or adventure. No, it's a necessary evil, a daily sacrifice that feels as mandatory as breathing but infinitely more miserable. The morning commute is bad enough—the bitter optimism of "Maybe today will be different" is swiftly obliterated by every selfie-stick wielding maniac, and agonizing speakerphone soliloquy that assails your senses with all the subtlety of a freight train. But it's the ride home that really drives you to the edge. The madness has escalated to such a degree that the perpetrators, now thoroughly drained by their 9-to-5 misadventures, have one singular goal: to be as disconnected to humanity as humanly possible while being as fully connected to their devices in as much as their wi-fi signal or data plan will allow.

They're exhausted. They're *spent*. The typical commuter, once a well-mannered individual clinging to the hope of some semblance of humanity, now morphs into a flesh-and-bone version of their phone—disconnected, indifferent, and blissfully unaware of how their actions are slowly driving you to the brink of madness. It's the final insult. The tired, beaten-down workers now transform into *full-on digital demons*, content to blast a podcast about their "self-care journey" at a volume that can only be described as "threatening."

The once-dignified process of sitting in silence and contemplating your existence or reading an actual book, (you remember those), has been replaced by the glaring brightness of another's screen glaring into your soul.

Chapter 2
Public Spaces & Private Places – Where 'Candid' Means Fifteen Takes and a Ring Light

Out here, authenticity is a performance, and spontaneity comes with a production schedule. Whether you're picnicking, people watching, or just trying to find the exit, rest assured—you're being curated into someone else's personal brand.

The Cult of the Constant Capture

Once upon a saner time—roughly six iPhone models, three TikTok trends, and one collective loss of dignity ago—public spaces were modest arenas of coexistence. People strolled. People browsed. People, dare I say it, conversed using actual vocal cords instead of barking into a Bluetooth headset like a deranged auctioneer selling crypto to ghosts. But that dusty, analog dream was violently hurled into the recycle bin of history, replaced by a ceaseless parade of clout-chasing charlatans, selfie-sycophants, and video-vultures all weaponizing their phones like social status sabers, hacking through basic human decency for likes, followers, and that sweet, sweet dopamine drip.

We no longer live. We document. We no longer feel. We filter. Life is not for living—it's for filming, framing, editing, and uploading. Authenticity has been amputated, replaced with a synthetic soul stitched together from hashtags and hot takes.

So go ahead. Film your lunch. Record your walk. Livestream your existential crisis. But remember: the world isn't just watching. The world is recording, too.

And we're all just unwilling extras in each other's bloated, boring, brain-numbing biopics. Welcome to reality—now with 100% less reality and 400% more ring lights.

Malls & Stores: Retail Therapy, Ruined Beyond Recognition

Welcome to your local shopping center—formerly a sanctuary of stale air conditioning, bad music, and consumer regret. Now? It's a fluorescent freak show, a hall of horrors curated by a generation of dead-eyed influencers treating every JCPenney and Sephora like the Met Gala. You came to buy socks. You left with PTSD and a cameo in three different TikToks.

The fragrance counter is now a battlefield of beauty blunders. One pseudo-celebrity, face spackled with seven layers of "natural glam," is locked in a gladiatorial match against her own reflection, mumbling motivational mantras into her camera as she fakes shock at a product she allegedly discovered "organically" five sponsored posts ago. Three steps away, a shirtless human protein shake does a dance-off in the menswear section, his abs glistening with desperation and Axe Body Spray. You don't know if it's performance art or a cry for help—and neither does he.

And you, poor soul, try to maneuver through aisles without becoming collateral content, you're met with the cold sting of a rogue ring light and the whiplash of a flailing selfie stick. Every aisle is booby-trapped with tripods, every corner infested with wannabe moguls narrating their "errand haul" like they're delivering a TED Talk on resilience. Store staff no longer ask if you need assistance—they ask if you're recording or just loitering uselessly.

At the food court, greasy anonymity has been replaced by gastro-glamour. Fries are fluffed, burgers are rotated, and ketchup is artfully drizzled for a better angle. You watch in horror as a man takes fifteen photos of his smoothie, only to throw it away because it "wasn't the right vibe." Across from him, a family of five hasn't eaten yet—because Mom needs footage of each of them pretending to enjoy the cardboard pizza while the kids starve and laugh on cue.

Intersections: Crosswalks of Cataclysmic Narcissism

Intersections used to be sites of cautious civility. Stop. Look. Listen. You know—basic survival skills. But now? They're cluttered catwalks for clowns caught in the tractor beam of their own cameras, strutting into traffic like they're God's gift to asphalt.

Behold: the light turns green, but no one moves. Why? Because a flock of fanny-packed fools has gathered mid-crosswalk to rehearse yet another TikTok dance routine, their limbs flailing like inflatable tube men on MDMA. Drivers honk, pedestrians fume, but the oblivious twits remain blissfully unaware, lost in the divine glow of their phone screens and the delusion that this 15-second spectacle will be their ticket to superstardom.

Behind them, a latte-sipping zombie drifts blindly through traffic, her eyes glued to a streaming video, her feet obeying no laws of physics or common sense. You slam on your brakes, save her life, and she doesn't even glance up—probably assumes the universe owes her an immortal bubble of safety. It's like Frogger, but everyone's the frog.

You watch as an elderly man—shopping bag in each trembling hand—tries to cross the street. He dodges a teen on a longboard filming his "daily vibes" montage and narrowly escapes being clotheslined by a woman live-streaming her existential crisis from the bike lane. The crosswalk is no longer a place to move from A to B. It's a stage, and you, unwilling extra, are in someone's opening credits whether you like it or not.

Stadiums & Concerts: Sacred Spaces of Sound, Smothered in Screens

You've paid a small fortune to see your favorite band live. You've stood in line, endured overpriced parking, and choked down stadium nachos that defy digestion. The lights dim, the crowd roars—and instantly, thousands of phones launch into the air like overexcited techy fireflies, each one blocking your view with the grace of a brick wall dipped in narcissism.

You came for music. You got a sea of sweaty hands, flickering screens, and Becky's vertical video with a side of shrill screaming. The man next to you is shouting over the chorus, narrating the experience into his phone like he's hosting a subpar podcast no one asked for. Behind you, someone FaceTimes a friend mid-song, holding the phone aloft so Aunt Mabel in Wichita can virtually ruin your night, too.

The performers beg—*beg*—the audience to put their phones down and live in the moment. They are met with booing, scoffing, and accusations of being "anti-freedom." Freedom, apparently, now means ruining real-life experiences in the name of collecting shaky footage no one will ever watch again.

By the third song, you've realized you'd get a better experience watching the livestream from home—at least there, no one's elbow is in your ear, and your soul isn't being slowly crushed by the sheer weight of secondhand embarrassment.

Crowded Streets & Parks: Scenic Routes of Suffering

Once, a city stroll meant absorbing the sounds of the street, watching dogs frolic in the park, maybe reflecting on life while dodging pigeons and existential dread. But now? Every sidewalk is a soundstage, every green space a godforsaken set for the most mediocre miniseries you never asked to star in.

A so-called 'motivational coach' has hijacked a bench with her tripod and two-ring light setup, preaching about "gratitude" while screaming at a pigeon that flew into her frame. Nearby, a shirtless man performs "primal yoga" in a fountain, flexing his spirituality at passersby while grunting like a wounded elk. Children are forbidden from playing because Mom's busy filming a slow-mo shot of her feet for her boho soul reel.

You try to sit. You're told to move—your normal human presence is "ruining the vibe." A pair of teens reenact a fake breakup for their YouTube channel while an older woman sobs into her salad nearby, ignored completely because she's not content-worthy. You, meanwhile, dodge a rogue drone piloted by someone who thinks aerial shots of pigeons and hot dog carts are cinematic masterpieces.

Airports, Ferries & Bus Stations: Where Sanity Comes to Die

Traveling is already a test of endurance, patience, and bladder control. But now? It's also a spectator sport. Airports are no longer transit hubs—they're reality show sets, each gate a glittering gladiator ring of live streams, vlog intros, and delusional airport OOTDs.

One guy with a ring light and a dead stare paced back and forth, repeating his intro for the tenth time: "Hey guys, welcome back to my travel channel…" No one welcomes him. No one subscribed. Across from him, a girl vlogged her every sneeze like it was breaking news. You learn far more about her sinus issues than you ever wanted.

Meet First-Class Business Barry — the apex predator of the productivity jungle. He boards the plane like he's the pilot, laptop already open before he sits, phone in one hand, watch vibrating like it's trying to escape his wrist, and three devices pinging in perfect corporate harmony. He's got deadlines, deliverables, and synergy, dammit! Every three minutes he sighs loudly, stares at his screen like he's decoding the Matrix, and mutters things like "We'll circle back." His watch buzzes, his phone dings, his laptop pings, and somehow, he still has time to make eye contact just long enough to silently inform you that he's more important than you'll ever be. He's quarterbacking the global economy from Seat 2A. Please, don't disturb him unless it's with artisanal espresso or a standing ovation.

On the ferry, some turtleneck-wearing poet films a slow-motion clip of his cappuccino while the sea splashes in the background. Meanwhile, toddlers scream, people vomit from motion sickness, and a middle-aged man tries to eat a sandwich in peace before being photobombed by a yoga influencer pretending to meditate against the railing.

The **long-haul bus trip** — the ultimate test of endurance, bladder control, and your ability to withstand the full-blown digital circus crammed into a Greyhound bus. It's every flavor of cell phone lunacy rolled into one vibrating, seat-kicking nightmare. You've got the **Cell Phone Senator** holding a press conference in row 12 about absolutely nothing important ("No, Carol, I said 20 pallets of mulch!"), the **Video Game Guru** in seat 8 hammering buttons like he's trying to launch a space shuttle, and the **TikTok Troupe** in the back rehearsing a dance routine that's 90% flailing and 10% catastrophic elbow contact. The ever-present **Selfie Savant.** A thousand selfies a week and growing. Add in a **YouTube Philosopher** monologuing at full blast about alien pyramids, and it's less of a bus ride, more of a mobile asylum powered by Wi-Fi and more poor life choices.

Weddings, Family Events & Kids' Birthdays: Emotional Extortion for the Algorithm

These events used to be about love, family, and frosting. Now? They're battlegrounds in the war for clout. Weddings are multi-angle, drone-shot disasters where every guest doubles as a cameraman. The bride barely makes it down the aisle without being flash blinded by Aunt Carol's iPad camera. The groom is halfway through his vows when he's interrupted by a live tweet.

The professional photographer is helpless against the swarm of smartphone saboteurs. The first kiss happens four times— because someone didn't get the angle. Grandma's birthday includes three takes of the candle blow because Sharon didn't like the lighting. She's 92 and exhausted. Sharon has a ring light and no soul.

Kid parties? Less about joy, more about optics. The cake is a prop. The presents are props. Even the kid is starting to suspect they're just a supporting actor in Mom's Instagram story. Joy is dead. Long live the content.

The self-appointed social media correspondent of the family reunion, live posting every handshake, half-hug, and awkward "Oh my God, you got so big!" like they're covering the Met Gala. She hasn't seen Cousin Linda in 40 years, but that won't stop her from shoving a phone in Linda's face mid-potato salad to snap a "candid" selfie captioned *#FamilyForever* — despite the fact that she misidentifies half of them as "probably Jim's kids?"

From malls to weddings, sidewalks to concerts, patios to Grandma's potato salad summit — no space is safe from the glowing grip of phone-fueled narcissism. Parks are now photo ops, family events are livestreams with cake, and restaurants? Just backdrops for bored people to scroll through photos of other meals they're not eating. Concerts are filmed entirely through shaky screens, and patios are graveyards of eye contact. It's not life — it's content with cutlery.

Chapter 3
Whining and Dining – A Prix Fixe of Public Narcissist

Today's specials include lukewarm linguine, shaken servers, and a generous drizzle of digital desperation. Also featured: a lovingly crafted faux restaurant menu and mission statement, because sarcasm pairs well with disappointment.

Coffee Shops and Cafes: Digital Dives of Social Degradation

Oh, coffee shops. Once the haven for introspective thinkers, casual conversations, and the gentle hum of espresso machines, now they've devolved into ground zero for digital narcissism. If there's one place where society's complete inability to enjoy a moment of peace and reflection is on full display, it's in the sterile, hyper-lit, faux-hipster aesthetic of today's coffee shop. What was once a cozy corner for reading or discussing ideas has been overrun by people who think that sitting in a café somehow makes them part of a "creative" subculture—except they've traded creativity for an unholy addiction to their phones, and instead of writing the next great novel, they're more likely to be meticulously crafting their next *perfect* Instagram post for the sole purpose of claiming their place in the digital spotlight.

You walk into a café, hoping for a brief respite from the endless digital noise of the outside world, only to find that everyone is glued to their screens, as though the mere presence of the Wi-Fi signal has turned them into zombies in a digital wasteland. The barista—who you suspect is probably also spending their downtime searching for gluten-free, non-dairy, organic almond butter on Etsy—is too busy checking their phone to even make eye contact. It's as if the very essence of human connection has been replaced by an array of beeps and clicks, with each ding from a phone serving as a jarring reminder that there's absolutely no chance of having a meaningful interaction in this particular space.

To your right, a woman sits alone at a small table, staring into the abyss of her phone, thumbs moving at light speed, as though she's in an Olympic event of texting with the emotional range of a brick wall. Her coffee sits untouched in front of her, growing colder by the minute as she minds her digital affairs. Is she texting a friend? Maybe. Is she dealing with something important? Probably not. She's probably just scrolling through a series of "stories," each hollower than the last, desperately trying to validate her existence by counting how many strangers clicked "like" on her perfectly curated latte art picture.

 But it's not just her—oh no, it's the entire café. Everyone, it seems, has their phone out. It's as if there's an invisible rulebook that says, *"If you're in a coffee shop, you must have a screen in front of you, or else your presence is irrelevant."* Every table is filled with the same monotonous scene: people with their heads down, hypnotically swiping through the endless barrage of meaningless content. Conversation? Gone. Connection? Absent. You could walk up to any one of these people and ask them how their day is going, and they'd respond as if you're the one who's interrupting their digital *bliss*, their eyes never fully lifting from the screen. *Don't you know they exist?*

Then, of course, there's the group of self-proclaimed "artists" or "entrepreneurs," sitting together, sipping overpriced coffees that cost more than your lunch, as they flick between their phones, pretending that their "work" is so critically important it can't be put down for even a minute. They talk in platitudes, feeding off one another's delusions of grandeur, speaking at length about the latest podcast episode they listened to or the social media influencer they're convinced will make them famous. Their fingers tap on their phones like they're doing something vital: updating their followers, posting memes, or curating their "brand" as if the world is hanging on their every digital move. They could be drafting the next business plan to save the world, but instead, they're drafting captions that will get the most "engagement." Meanwhile, they share nothing of substance with each other—no deep conversations, no real connection. They could be best friends, but they might as well be strangers, because they're all too absorbed in their screens to share anything that matters. In fact, their idea of an interaction is sharing a "like" on an Instagram post and giving a thumbs-up emoji in a group text, because, hey, *that's meaningful*, right?

Behind you, a man is holding a Zoom meeting, which, in this coffee shop, might as well be a public performance. He's speaking loudly—too loudly—into his phone, while somehow pretending he isn't in a public space. His voice echoes through the café like a booming alarm, drowning out any last traces of ambiance that the place once held. "Can you hear me?" he asks, but it's clear he's asking this question not because he's concerned about whether his colleagues can hear him, but because he wants *everyone* to hear him. He repeats his points over and over, as though the people sitting around him are all part of his virtual meeting. He continues on, oblivious to the frustrated glances thrown his way from people who just want to sip their coffee in peace. Why should he care about the physical world around him? His meeting is the only thing that matters right now. The noise from his call is as intrusive as it is completely unnecessary.

And then, there's the group of friends who meet up under the guise of "catching up," but really, they're just sitting side by side, lost in their individual feeds. They make occasional eye contact, smile awkwardly, and then go back to scrolling. At best, they'll look up from their phones long enough to say, "Oh, I saw that post you liked." But the real question is—why? Why even meet up in person if the only connection you're fostering is through the sterile, inhuman glow of a phone screen? At this point, you're not even in the same room anymore. Everyone's physically present, but mentally? They're halfway across the world. The beauty of a shared meal, the joy of real-time conversation, the comfort of being surrounded by people who truly see you—none of that matters when the screen is the *only* thing that can hold their attention. Maybe they think they're just doing "the thing" everyone else is doing—filling their idle hours with digital noise—but the truth is, they're robbing themselves of real moments, of real connection. They are mere shadows of the people they used to be, consumed by the need for external validation, constantly seeking approval from a digital world that doesn't care about them in the slightest.

You look around, and it's like the very essence of human interaction is slowly being bled out of the room, one mindless scroll at a time. Gone are the days of overhearing a pleasant conversation or enjoying a few moments of quiet contemplation with your coffee. Now, it's a competition to see who can ignore reality the most convincingly. Someone might make a passing comment about the weather or the ridiculousness of some viral TikTok challenge, but it's all hollow noise—something to say to fill the void of their own inability to engage with their surroundings in a meaningful way. Nobody's interested in the weather. Nobody cares about the latest viral sensation, because they've all been consumed by the machine that is social media, each one trapped in their own cycle of obsession. It's not real life. It's an endless game of who can appear more interesting while doing absolutely nothing of substance.

The café that was once a place of inspiration and warmth now reeks of apathy and superficiality, a place where souls go to rot while their fingers endlessly tap and swipe away, leaving only the echoes of missed opportunities and wasted potential behind them. But who cares, right? As long as they're on their phones, pretending to be busy, pretending to be important, it's all worth it. Never mind the fact that they're more disconnected than ever before. Never mind the fact that they're missing the beauty of the world around them, the real moments that make life worth living. As long as their feed is updated, their validation intact, they'll carry on, numb to the world they've locked themselves out of.

Bars and Nightclubs: The Real Party is in the Feed

The sacred night out—once a vibrant, joyous escape where the clinking of glasses, the pounding of bass, and the sweet rush of drunken freedom filled the air. But now? Now, it's a digital disaster zone, where people care more about how their night looks through a filter than how it actually feels in real time. The once-thriving temples of social interaction, camaraderie, and uninhibited fun have morphed into nothing more than live-streamed cathedrals of narcissism, where the only thing that matters is capturing the *perfect shot* to show the world that, yes, your life is just as exciting as the influencers you follow. Forget real conversations, spontaneous dances, or the serendipity of meeting new people—it's all about how you can document every second of the evening for your social media followers, most of whom wouldn't recognize you in person even if you tripped over them in the middle of the dance floor.

Let's start with the bar. The bar—a place that once invited loud, joyful conversations and spontaneous connection—now hums with the gentle, robotic sound of the ever-present "click, click, click" of phones being used to snap photos of drinks. You thought you were coming here to unwind, to forget the grind of the week. But no. Instead, you're treated to an endless parade of self-important people who seem to think that their one-off cocktail is worthy of a photoshoot. A woman, dressed in a crop top that somehow costs more than your rent, orders a drink. It arrives—an abomination of muddled fruit, crushed ice, and neon-colored syrup designed solely to make it look good on Instagram. But does she take a sip? Does she even care what the drink tastes like? Of course not. She raises her phone above her head like she's capturing a once-in-a-lifetime event, asking the bartender to "just hold the glass a little to the left, for the perfect lighting." Her phone is the real star here, not the drink, and she knows it. You wonder if anyone even knows how to enjoy a drink without broadcasting it to the world.

Meanwhile, the guy next to you—the one who's already had *way* too many tequila shots—squints at the bartender like he's trying to make sense of an ancient hieroglyph. He's not here to chat. He's not even aware of the people around him. What he's here for is the *perfect* video, a slow-motion shot of him taking a sip, throwing his head back, and dramatically wiping his mouth afterward like he's the star of a tequila commercial. His friend?

He's not helping. His friend is holding the camera, as if he's directing a high-budget Hollywood production. If you're lucky, the camera will catch the sweat dripping from the guy's brow as he stumbles to hold his balance. But, hey, who cares about reality when you can create a curated version of it, right?

Then, of course, there's the digital drinker's worst nightmare: the group photo. No one ever remembers how many shots they've taken, but everyone remembers to take that group photo that will be posted on social media, because, apparently, if it doesn't exist online, did it even happen? It's a spectacle—a ritualistic scene where everyone, no matter how intoxicated or disheveled, lines up with strained smiles, fighting the urge to vomit while holding their drinks as if they're participating in some absurd cult ceremony. "Can we redo that? I didn't look cute enough," says one of the individuals, all while their friends argue about which filter makes them look more tanned, "flawless," or "glowing." Real human interaction is nowhere to be found in these moments. You can almost feel the soul-crushing weight of everyone's desperate need for validation hanging in the air. If no one posts about it, did the fun even occur?

Now, onto the nightclub—the once-glorious house of pulsating music, wild dancing, and the kind of carefree joy that only a night of sweat and bass could provide. But now? Now it's just a flashing neon nightmare, where everyone is staring at their phones instead of each other. The music? It's merely background noise, drowned out by the incessant clicking and swiping. The dance floor? Forget it. You look around and realize that half of the "dancers" are more interested in capturing the *perfect* shot of themselves under the strobe lights than actually moving to the rhythm. The real party, it seems, is in their Instagram stories, not in their bodies or the moments they could be living. How much better would the night be if they just let loose and actually felt the music instead of waiting for the right lighting for their profile picture? But no, they're too busy adjusting their angles, checking their reflection in the darkened glass of the bar, and making sure their fit is *just right* for the feed. At this point, you wonder if any of them even know what it means to dance, to get lost in the sound, to feel the thrum of the bass in their chest. Apparently, that's a relic of the past, something people used to do before the age of digital self-aggrandizement.

And don't get me started on the *VIP section*, where the truly egregious behavior reaches a fever pitch. The lights are dimmed to near total darkness, and it's less of a "club" and more of a *contest*—a contest to see who can pose the hardest, hold the champagne bottle the highest, and scream the loudest into the void of their own self-importance. People order expensive bottles of liquor they don't even drink, simply because it looks *good* on their social feed. They'll even ask for a bottle to be delivered with sparklers because—what's the point of having money if you don't flaunt it in everyone's face? The music? Unimportant. The conversation? Nonexistent. It's the spectacle that counts—who can make their life look like the most glamorous, most exclusive one on social media? The nightclub has ceased being a place for revelry; it's now a stage for self-indulgent displays of wealth and status. No one's dancing anymore, because they're too busy flexing their disposable income for the likes of strangers who couldn't care less about their existence.

To top it all off, a new breed of clubgoers has emerged: the influencers. You can spot them a mile away. They're the ones who wander the club with their phones raised, filming themselves with all the energy of a high-budget fashion shoot. They're often accompanied by a group of similarly "styled" people who are more concerned with *how* their drinks are being served than actually consuming the alcohol. The night is an endless parade of "candid" moments—each one more staged than the last—where the real point is not the party itself, but how the party can be sold to their followers. Every toast, every laugh, every "spontaneous" dance move is meticulously documented for the world to see. There's no joy, no freedom— just a constant need to project an image of happiness, an image that is as artificial as the filters they use to enhance their "fun."

And you? You're stuck in the middle of it all, desperately trying to find a way to enjoy the night while surrounded by people who seem to have forgotten that it's not about the *perfect* angle, but the actual, messy joy of being alive, of experiencing something in real time. But no. The real party is no longer in the club—it's in the posts, the stories, and the desperate pursuit of digital validation. Welcome to the modern night-out nightmare, where everyone is too busy capturing the moment to actually live it.

Pubs and Patios: An Instagram Feed of Outside Eateries and Plates of Disillusionment

Once upon a time—not all that long ago—pubs and patios were havens of relaxed joy. Places to unwind, connect, and, dare I say it, *converse* over a plate of nachos or a cold pint. There was laughter, impromptu debates, boisterous cheers during a game, flirtations under string lights, and the occasional drunken rendition of "Bohemian Rhapsody" that united strangers like a sacred hymn. But those days are dead. Buried beneath a six-foot-deep grave of hashtags, geotags, influencer filters, and the slow, digital death of shared reality.

Now, pubs and patios are little more than outdoor studios—open-air backdrops for social media spectacles. Places where the drinks are warm, the food is cold, and nobody cares as long as the photo *slaps*. The clientele isn't there to savor the flavor or enjoy the vibe. No, they're here to pretend. To stage their little online dramas where the lighting is golden, the smile is frozen, and the entire evening is manufactured for likes. The only thing being served is delusion.

Let's begin with the grand entrance—the Influencer Stroll. She arrives in designer sunglasses that weigh more than her dignity, draped in an outfit designed more for visibility than functionality. It's 2:30 PM on a Tuesday, but she's dressed like she's about to walk the red carpet of an award show nobody invited her to. Her friend—equally overdressed and underwhelming—has been assigned the role of camera operator. "Wait—stand back, I want to get the trees in the shot," she says, as if capturing the withered urban shrubbery in the background will somehow lend her life the elegance of a Tuscan vineyard.

They choose their table not based on comfort, or view, or temperature, but based on which direction the light hits their skin. After five minutes of shuffling seats, they settle on the "golden hour" angle—the sacred direction that offers maximum jawline definition and minimum exposure of real pores. Before even glancing at a menu, they've already taken no fewer than twelve photos. Of what, you ask? Themselves. Their hands. Their hair fluttering in the artificially summoned breeze of a friend waving a napkin just off camera. The patio could be on fire, and they'd still be angling their phones to crop out the flames.

And then the food arrives. Oh, sweet summer child, you thought they came to eat? How precious. The moment the server puts the plate down, the table becomes a runway. Phones rise in unison, as if in prayer. Angles are checked. Forks are rearranged—not for taste, but for aesthetic. A sprig of parsley is scooted two millimeters left. Someone rotates the plate three times to "find its good side." Meanwhile, the food, once warm and worthy of taste buds, dies a slow, camera-flash-drenched death. No one dares take the first bite until all parties have completed their 4-part "foodie reel." God forbid you eat a single fry before it's been lovingly documented, edited, and uploaded to a story captioned with something like: *"Vibes.* 🦋 *#brunchgoals #outdoorEATS #yum."* The only thing less authentic than the filter is the enjoyment being faked on their faces.

Look around. You'll see another group of "friends" who, if you eavesdrop just a little (and how can you not—they're speaking at full volume for the benefit of their microphones), are *not* catching up. They're filming a "Patio Talk Q&A" for TikTok. The topic? "Why I ghost people." Riveting stuff. One girl, staring dead into her front camera, launches into an impassioned monologue about "setting boundaries" while a pigeon performs a slow suicide dive into her untouched avocado toast. Not that she notices. She's too busy making sure her hair falls just so.

Her friends? They nod robotically, checking their own angles between feigned expressions of emotional depth. A guy across the table pulls out a ring light. A. RING. LIGHT. For brunch. For daylight. For whatever remains of our crumbling civilization.

Meanwhile, those who dared to show up for actual *connection* are left floundering. The sad souls on actual dates—where one person puts their phone down and tries to engage in genuine conversation—watch their efforts die with each distracted scroll from their partner. "Sorry, just checking something," says the date, who's clearly not checking anything. They're texting a group chat about how boring this is, while simultaneously watching someone else's patio reel to see if they missed a better spot. You could say something brilliant, something deeply moving, and it would be met with a distracted "Huh? Oh, sorry—what were you saying?" as they upload another selfie with the caption *"So present rn ♡."* The irony alone should be enough to cause spontaneous combustion.

Patios were meant to be that sweet middle ground between the indoors and the outside—a liminal space where conversation flowed as freely as the pints, and people *noticed* each other. But now they're stages. Runways. Self-congratulatory sets for lifestyle theatre, where the audience is invisible and the actors are all pretending not to act. Even the servers know it. Watch them try to drop off a plate while dodging three tripods and a TikTok dance in progress. The server says, "Can I get you anything else?" and the response is, "Yeah—can you take a photo of us?" Their eyes die a little more each time.

And let us not forget the live-story broadcasters—the people who narrate every bite, every breeze, every clink of glass as if they're the protagonist in a reality show no one's watching. They'll stare into their front camera and say things like, "Just enjoying this beautiful day with my soul sisters," while the friend they're referring to stares blankly at a pigeon fighting a napkin in the corner. Real connection? Nonexistent. Shared memories? Only if they show up in Time Hop.

In the end, what was once a joyfully chaotic, occasionally tipsy celebration of food, friends, and fresh air has become a painstakingly curated scene of digital desperation. A place where plates are prettier than they are edible, conversations are replaced by captions, and the only clinking glasses you hear are followed by, "Hold on, let me boomerang that."

Welcome to the patio—where the sun is warm, the food is cold, and the people are emotionally unavailable, eternally editing their lives for an audience that's not paying attention.

Restaurants: The Fine Dining Funeral March, with a Side of Wi-Fi and Emotional Bankruptcy

Let us now eulogize the restaurant. Not the fast-food drive-thru or the grab-and-go salad bar, but the *restaurant*—the dimly lit, soft-jazz-playing temple of togetherness. A place where couples once leaned over candlelit tables to whisper secrets, where families laughed over pasta, and friends clinked glasses in joyous reunion. It was a place of flavor and feeling. Of artistry plated in porcelain. Of human warmth, cozy lighting, and the gentle background hum of shared moments.

And now? Now it's a photography studio with overpriced appetizers.

The restaurant of today no longer serves meals—it serves *content opportunities*. The clientele doesn't want to be fed; they want to be *followed*. They don't arrive hungry for food—they arrive starved for *engagement*. And no one is hungrier than the foodie influencer, the high priest of performative consumption, who has single handedly turned a medium-rare steak into a support beam in their house of online delusion.

Let's talk about the **atmosphere**, or what's left of it after it's been obliterated by ring lights, impromptu iPhone flashes, and live commentary echoing across what was once a serene dining room. You sit down at your candlelit table, hoping for a relaxing evening. Instead, you're treated to a one-woman photoshoot happening two tables over. She's standing on her chair—yes, *on* the chair—hovering above her entrée like a hawk with a 14 Pro Max. Her phone case sparkles like a cursed talisman. Her voice pierces the air: "Oh my GOD, the *lighting* in here is SO BAD."

Of course it is. Because this is a restaurant, not a sound stage for your unremarkable life.

And pity the poor waitstaff. Once noble ambassadors of hospitality, they are now glorified tech support and part-time photographers for entitled table trolls. "Could you take a picture of us?"—once an innocent request, now an unholy ritual. The server must crouch, angle, frame, and retake the shot no fewer than six times while the diners grimace with the kind of joyless vanity usually reserved for passport photos. God forbid the server doesn't understand your preferred angle. "Umm, can you try it again but like, from lower? No, lower. Like squat-level. Perfect. Can you also blur the background?"

Yes, Brenda. Let me grab my DSLR, step into this cinematic fantasy of yours, and channel my inner Scorsese while your carbonara congeals.

And we *mustn't* forget the **Wi-Fi crisis**. Before the menu is even opened, before a single crumb has been broken, a desperate question is asked: "Do you have Wi-Fi?" Not because anyone is trying to work remotely or stream a movie—no, no. The Instagram stories need to go up **now**, and their data plan is tragically inadequate. People clutch their phones like they're drowning and the Wi-Fi password is a life preserver. They flag down the server—not for recommendations, not for drink orders, but because the signal is "super weak in this corner." Some even demand to be moved. Not for a better view, but for a stronger connection. Romantic, isn't it?

And once the Wi-Fi connects—sweet digital Jesus—the real performance begins. You'll see someone order a dish not for its flavor, but for its photogenic potential. "What's your most *aesthetic* plate?" is now a legitimate question posed to people who went to culinary school. And once that photogenic plate arrives—let's say, a beautifully arranged braised lamb shank—it will be left untouched for ten minutes as it's rotated, photographed, and filtered like a modeling agency headshot. By the time the first bite is taken, the meat is colder than the heart of the person posting, and the mashed potatoes have the consistency of concrete.

Oh, and don't expect to enjoy the background music. That tasteful playlist of jazz, classical guitar, or ambient café tunes is routinely obliterated by the *external soundtrack* of FaceTime calls at full volume, TikTok videos playing with no headphones (because apparently, those are optional now), and "vlog-style" narration from diners recapping their entire day for an audience that, if we're being honest, doesn't care. You'll hear things like,

"Hey guys, so we're at this cute little bistro on the corner—here's the menu—hold on, let me flip the camera—ugh, the lighting is so trash—okay, now you can kinda see it..." Meanwhile, across the room, an actual couple is trying to celebrate their anniversary in peace, which is harder than ever since their ambiance is being stolen by the verbal diarrhea of someone named *Kenzleigh* who thinks the world needs to know she ordered fries instead of the truffle risotto.

The dining room used to be a symphony of sounds—clinking glasses, murmured conversation, the occasional burst of laughter. Now, it's a cacophony of digital chaos. Notifications *ding*, screens glow, and laughter is replaced with silence, save for the hollow tapping of thumbs on glass. People aren't reacting to each other—they're reacting to their screens. Someone's telling a story, but nobody's listening. One person's showing photos of their new puppy, and everyone else is "just checking something real quick." Nobody's *here*. Everyone's *somewhere else*, virtually multitasking themselves out of the human experience.

And heaven help the restaurant that tries to resist. The moment a place bans phones or asks for a "no photography" policy? Chaos. Uproar. A smear campaign on Yelp. "They wouldn't even let me film my unboxing video for the bread basket! So rude!" These people want immersive experiences, as long as those experiences can be paused, edited, uploaded, and monetized.

The result? A complete collapse of the dining experience. The food is still good—sometimes even *amazing*—but nobody's tasting it. The ambiance might be charming, but it's drowned beneath the click of a camera shutter. The people are present in body but absent in spirit. You could swap them out with mannequins, and no one would notice, as long as their phones were still active.

So here we are sitting in dim rooms, surrounded by digitally flickering candles and silent diners, all bathed in the eerie blue light of their screens. We've traded palate for popularity, experience for exposure, and flavor for filters. Restaurants aren't places to connect anymore—they're content farms. Human warmth has been replaced by artificial engagement, and the only thing truly being consumed is your sense of self.

The modern version of "Putting on the Ritz".

Chapter 4
The Fork and Scroll
Where the Signal's Stronger Than the Human Connection

Welcome to the House of Phones, where the ambiance is filtered, the conversation is on airplane mode, and the only thing getting full service is your device. This is a five-course feast of digital dysfunction set in the last remaining places once reserved for eye contact, laughter, and—dare we say it—actual interaction.

Enjoy, a steaming appetizer of influencers rearranging cutlery for the perfect shot, a main course of group diners with zero dialogue, and a dessert so cold it might just ghost you before you taste it. Our mission is clear: turn every restaurant, bar, patio, café, and social nook into a Wi-Fi-enabled house of horrors.

Welcome to The Fork & Scroll

A Restaurant Concept So Horrific, I Had to Invent It

I never wanted to open a restaurant. Let's start there.

In fact, the very idea of curating a menu for a clientele that hasn't made eye contact with another human since the invention of the selfie stick fills me with nausea only rivaled by the scent of truffle oil in a hot car. But alas, I am merely a product of my time—a time when the dopamine-starved masses need a food venue that exists less for nourishment and more for narrative.

Thus, I give you *The Fork & Scroll*, the future of dining—because who the hell cares about flavor when you can filter? Here, you don't eat because you're hungry. You eat because your followers are. Your appetite is for attention. Your cravings? Validation. And I'm here to help you plate it.

Every dish on this menu has been triple-tested: once for taste (briefly), once for visual flair (extensively), and once for how well it pairs with a heavy-handed caption like "So blessed 🍴✨🌀." Our servers? Don't ask if they're certified in hospitality—ask how many TikTok transitions they've mastered while balancing a tray of $19 mocktails. Our kitchen? Less a place for culinary art, more a backlit stage where emotionally unavailable food meets emotionally unstable diners.

Let's be clear: I've built this place not out of love, but out of surrender. A white-flag-waving response to the horror I've witnessed—people ordering five entrees "for content" and leaving them to rot while they scroll. Diners live-streaming first dates with the charisma of wet cardboard. Groups of friends sitting in stony silence, each one fondling their phones like it's a beloved pet instead of the main reason none of them have spoken in three years.

This menu? It's satire dressed as a service. It's performance art with a balsamic reduction. It's the final, flaming nail in the coffin of meaningful human connection, gift-wrapped in edible gold leaf and chased with a vegan bone broth chaser. So yes, welcome. Sit down, plug in, disconnect from everything that matters, and enjoy your meal. Don't forget to tag us. Oh, and the Wi-Fi password is **#EATYOURHEARTOUT**

(Caps matter. Much like your soul, our signal is fragile.)

Bon appétit, or whatever emoji-riddled nonsense passes for that now.

📷 THE Fork & Scroll

"Where You Don't Eat to Live, You Eat to Post.

APPETIZERS (a.k.a. Engagement Bait)

- **The Hashtag Hash**
- Crispy golden potatoes, aggressively sprinkled with smoked paprika and performative parsley. Served in a miniature cast-iron skillet you're 100% going to steal for future #brunch pics.
- *Garnished with a QR code to link your followers directly to your food blog.*
- **Clout Cakes**
- Trio of bite-sized crab cakes, one topped with edible gold leaf, one with activated charcoal, and one with

existential dread. Comes with three dipping sauces and zero emotional depth.

- *Pair with an air of superiority.*
- **Influencer Nachos**
- Blue corn chips arranged in the shape of your initials, drenched in vegan queso and shredded D-list celebrity relevance. Topped with hand-massaged avocado flown in from an overpriced farmer's market.
- *Feeds one. Looks like it feeds eight.*
- **Faux Gras Flatbread**

  Duck-free, duck-fat-free, duck less "foie gras" spread over

- micro-arugula and laminated narcissism. Each order includes a tiny mirror so you can watch yourself chew.

MAIN COURSES (a.k.a. Posts with Purpose)

- **The Avocado Toast of Eternal Emptiness**

  Thick-cut artisanal sourdough buried beneath a pile of overripe avocado, motivational microgreens, edible flowers, and a strategically cracked poached egg.

  Served with a free trial of therapy.

- **Linguine for the Likes**

  Al dente noodles tossed in a creamy garlic guilt sauce, garnished with shaved truffle you'll pretend to recognize. Served by a waiter who whispers "You're stunning" every time you boomerang your fork twirl.

The Braised Lamb of Self-Importance

Slow-cooked lamb shank in a red wine jus so dramatic it should come with a trigger warning. Sits atop a bed of roasted vegetables arranged to spell out "YOU'RE WELCOME."

Ask your server to hold a ring light over your shoulder during your dinner vlog.

The Keto Karma Bowl

Grass-fed beef, zoodles, and shattered ambition over a bed of kale shrapnel. Comes with a side of smugness and a link to your intermittent fasting blog.

- **Sad Salmon Selfie**

- Sous-vide salmon served tepid to give you time to record a "taste test" video with eight cuts, two zoom-ins, and a fake surprise face. Plated with a single asparagus spear stabbed dramatically through a lemon wedge.

DESSERTS (a.k.a. #SweetLikeMe)

- **The Crème Brû-lie For Attention**

Caramelized sugar crust torched tableside while you film yourself mouthing a trending audio. The custard underneath is mediocre at best, but your reaction video will be *fire*.

- **The Gelato of Gentle Disappointment**

Three scoops: Charcoal Vanilla (for aesthetics), Earl Grey Ennui, and Matcha Melancholy. Served in a golden waffle cone you won't eat because "you're just here for the vibe."

- **Deconstructed S'mores of the Soul**

  Artisanal graham cracker rubble, scorched marshmallow fluff smear, and ethically ambiguous chocolate drizzle. Comes with a free tweet that reads "OMG this dessert just changed my life 🔥."

- **The Infinite Cheesecake Loop**

  Mini cheesecake cube resting in the center of a swirling raspberry coulis spiral, carefully engineered to loop endlessly on Boomerang.

- *More loop than cake.*

SPECIALTY DRINKS (a.k.a. Liquid Validation)

- **The Iced Oat-Spresso Manifesto**

  Cold brew that tastes like regret, mixed with organic oat milk and served in a glass jar with motivational quote decals. Comes with a biodegradable straw and a long caption about "living your truth."

- **Matcha Made in Heaven**

  Ceremonial-grade matcha whisked by a barista wearing a fedora and silent judgment. Comes with a small flower crown you're required to wear while sipping.

- **The Detoxifying Life Crisis**

  Charcoal lemonade served in a prism-shaped glass, with an unnecessary sprig of rosemary and a sidecar of denial. Tastes like filtered despair.

- **Blue Tonic Elixir of Enlightenment**

  Butterfly pea flower tonic with a splash of gin and a splash of delusion. Changes color when stirred, unlike your personality.

- **The Aperol Ego Spritz** Aperol, prosecco, soda, and inflated self-worth. Garnished with a dehydrated orange slice and a selfie stick.

Ⓝ NOTE FROM THE KITCHEN:

Please do not eat anything before your server has finished taking professional-level portraits of your dish from six angles. Ring lights are available at each table. Tip your server *in exposure*.

Chapter 5
Swiped Left on Sanity
The Love Algorithm That Ghosted Humanity

Ah, modern romance. The sacred search for connection, now proudly brought to you by servers, swipes, and sociopathic small talk. Once upon a time, love was something found in glances, conversations, and perhaps the occasional slow dance under questionable lighting. Now, it's sourced through a meat market of filtered selfies, emoji fluency, and the emotional range of a stapler. Welcome to dating in the

The Apocalypse Swipe, Tap, Repeat

Behold the dating app: humanity's most brilliant innovation for ensuring everyone is simultaneously too accessible and completely unavailable. You upload a photo—one that bears only a distant relation to your actual face—add three adjectives that sound deep ("adventurous," "witty," and "sapiosexual," because nothing says you're intellectually elite like pretending to get turned on by dictionaries), and then you let the roulette of lust begin.

Profiles fly by in a narcissistic blur. There's Jeff with a dead fish, Karen with a yoga pose, someone whose name is an emoji, and a slew of gym mirror selfies that scream, "I love myself, and I might tolerate you." Want to meet someone authentic? Good luck. Dating apps are carefully curated theatres of delusion, where every profile pic is a lie, every bio a résumé of half-truths, and every message an attempt to delay actual human interaction for as long as technologically possible.

The algorithm matches you with someone who "shares your interests," which apparently means they, too, once listed "The Office" as their favorite show. You both swipe right, a digital spark is ignited, and then—nothing. Just dead air. Because why speak when you can validate yourself with a match and move on to the next dopamine hit?

And then there are the serial swipers—those digital junkies who treat Tinder like a video game. They swipe right on everyone, fishing for matches like bored CEOs flipping through résumés. These aren't hopeful romantics. These are swipe-hoarders, gobbling up matches like social currency, only to never message, never meet, never move. You, dear reader, were just another pixel in their quest for virtual self-esteem.

First Dates, First Disappointments

You agree to meet. You pick a place with lighting forgiving enough to smooth over the gap between expectation and reality. You arrive, and there they are: 5 inches shorter, 10 years older, 30 pounds heavier, and about as charismatic as a damp sponge. They wave, and you force a smile while screaming internally.

They spend the evening glued to their phone, occasionally making eye contact the way someone might check a smoke detector—quickly, and with suspicion. They're not rude, they say, they're just "so busy." Busy texting, swiping, scrolling. You try to start a conversation, but the phone pings. They glance. You're mid-sentence, talking about your dog dying, but no matter. Someone just posted a Reel.

You sit there, reduced to a live-action background prop for their social feed. At one point they film their cocktail, then themselves, then you, uninvited, saying "#datenight" with the enthusiasm of someone announcing a root canal. You excuse yourself to the bathroom, not because you need to go, but because you need to scream into your own hands for a solid minute.

You return, and the nightmare continues. They ask you what your star sign is and immediately judge your entire existence based on celestial nonsense. They show you TikToks mid-meal. They mention their therapist in the same breath as their cat. They interrupt you to post a story, ask the waiter to take a photo from "a flattering angle," and argue with you about whether pineapple belongs on pizza like it's a philosophical debate.

Ghosting & Breadcrumbing: The New Romance Languages

Remember when people broke up with dignity? Maybe a phone call, maybe a weepy meet-up in a park? Now, they disappear like Vegas magicians. Ghosting is the default setting for digital cowards who can't be bothered to write, "Not feeling it." Instead, they vanish into thin bandwidth, leaving you wondering if you said something wrong, or if they died in a tragic influencer accident.

Breadcrumbing is even worse—the passive-aggressive sibling of ghosting. That's when someone keeps you just interested enough to prevent you from moving on, tossing you the occasional "Hey stranger" like you're a lab rat being conditioned for disappointment. They don't want you. They don't want *anyone*. They just need a safety net for the nights their internet connection is too weak to stream porn.

Even worse, they might double-tap your photo from three weeks ago—just enough to leave you spiraling in confusion. Was it an accident? A sign? A cruel social experiment? Spoiler alert: it was none of the above. It was just digital debris left by someone with the attention span of a goldfish and the empathy of a toaster.

Romantic Red Flags, Digitally Delivered

So, you somehow end up in something resembling a relationship. You text, you share memes, you tag each other in videos about couples who own matching sweatpants. But the signs are there: they reply to your messages with "k," which in emotional maturity terms is basically a slap with a cold fish.

They take three hours to respond but are always online. They cancel plans with, "Just feeling meh."

They make you take 37 photos of them in front of a brick wall, then say you're "not getting the lighting right." You suggest something fun for the weekend, and they reply, "Can we just chill?"—code for "stare at our phones in the same room like emotionally distant siblings."

When they do show affection, it's through emojis and reaction gifs. They say "ily" instead of "I love you," and even that feels like a contractual obligation. You ask them what they want out of this relationship, and they shrug. You ask them if they see a future together, and they ask if you've seen the new Instagram filter that makes your eyes look like a cat's.

The Filtered Façade: Love in a World of Lies

One of the great joys of digital dating is discovering that the person you've been talking to for weeks is actually a hologram of their former self. Online, they're witty, engaging, passionate about art and social justice. In person, they speak only in TikTok audio clips and think Monet is a brand of perfume.

Their profile photo? From 2014. Their job title? Aspirational. Their travel pics? Carefully cropped to hide the fact they never left the resort. You find yourself nodding along as they retell an Instagram story, they posted last night like it's a personal anecdote.

Eventually, you become so numb to the charade that you start doing it too. You pretend to laugh at memes you don't understand. You pretend you're fine when they take a phone call mid-conversation. You pretend your relationship isn't just two people pretending to have a relationship. And when it inevitably ends, you delete the apps for a week in protest—until loneliness and peer pressure lure you back like a moth to a flaming dumpster.

Post-Love Purgatory: The Emotional Aftermath

After the ghosting, the mediocre sex, the emotional unavailability wrapped in sarcasm and avocado toast, you reflect. You wonder if maybe you're the problem. You're not. Society is. You were born in the wrong era—one where people called each other, showed up on time, and didn't end conversations with an eggplant emoji.

You consider therapy, but your therapist is also on Bumble and once matched with you. You consider moving to a remote cabin in the woods, but you'd still get Tinder notifications from someone three kilometers away looking to "vibe." So instead, you accept your fate. You become a dating monk, observing the chaos from afar, collecting horror stories like Pokémon, and warning others of the perils that await them on Hinge.

Conclusion: Love, in the Time of Wi-Fi

We've traded subtlety for swipe speed, patience for push notifications, and romance for reach.

But maybe there's still hope. Maybe, just maybe, the next time you match with someone, you'll both put down your phones, look each other in the eye, and have a real conversation. Or maybe not. Maybe they'll just send you a Bit Moji, say "lol," and vanish forever. Either way, welcome to the future of love. Batteries not included.

Chapter 6
The Digital Parent — Raising Children in the Age of Digital Neglect

The modern marvel of parenting, where the first rule of child-rearing isn't "love and nurture," but "keep them distracted so I can scroll through my Instagram feed uninterrupted." Parenting in the age of smartphones is a special breed of neglect, one where the child's need for attention is only rivaled by the parent's desperate need to check their text messages. These are the people who mistakenly believe that handing their kid an iPad is the epitome of responsible parenting, as if 18 apps and 12 hours of YouTube videos somehow replace the occasional heartfelt "How was your day, sweetie?"

Let's begin with the harrowing reality of the digital babysitter. You know the parent — the one who hands their toddler a smartphone like it's a cookie and a glass of milk. Here, kiddo, play a game, swipe at the screen for half an hour while I scroll through my Instagram feed, pretending I'm interested in the memes that my college roommate posted in 2012. It's like they think their kid is suddenly a technological prodigy just because they can open an app and stare blankly at flashing colors for an hour. The child's cognitive development? Meh. As long as they're entertained. Who needs face-to-face conversation when you've got a device that'll hold their attention long enough for you to finish your third cup of coffee?

And oh, the joys of watching a "parent" pretend they're actually present in their child's life. The sheer audacity of these phone-addicted mummies and daddies, who look up from their glowing screens just long enough to grunt, "Yeah, sure, that sounds fun," when their child asks if they can play. You can practically hear the exhaustion in their voice — the mental fatigue of having to give even the smallest iota of attention to their offspring when TikTok is calling. Parenting used to be about guidance, wisdom, and the occasional bedtime story. Now? It's about strategically planning when to hand off the device so you can have an uninterrupted five minutes to swipe through other people's vacations and coffee shop selfies.

But it doesn't stop there. Oh, no. There's an entire generation of parents who believe that their child's screen time is simply an extension of their own screen time. They're not aware that they've essentially abdicated their role as a caregiver, as they hand their child an iPad at every possible opportunity. "Oh, don't worry," they say with a sigh of relief, "Johnny's playing his educational game." No, he's not. Johnny is learning how to mindlessly scroll through an endless feed of irrelevant content, watching unboxing videos and playing games designed by people who couldn't care less about his long-term emotional development. But hey, at least you can check your social media without any interruptions, right?

Let's not forget the brilliance of giving your child their own device to keep them entertained while you get your precious digital "me time." Ah, yes, let's equip them with a $500 tablet, as though that's the only way to foster independent learning and creativity. Sure, who needs blocks, crayons, or actual social interaction when you can hand them a device that will immediately start feeding them endless

advertisements disguised as games? Better yet, why not buy them a subscription to some ridiculous online learning tool that promises to develop their mind for $9.99 a month? What a win! Who cares if they never learn the joys of nature, conversation, or using their imagination? At least you don't have to hear them ask for a snack every five minutes.

Then, there's the ever-prevalent digital screen at family gatherings. Oh, yes, this is where the magic happens: the "family" dinner. Nothing says "quality time" like sitting at a table where every single person — including the children — is glued to their respective screens, pretending to be interested in the latest text or social media update, while the turkey gets cold and the mashed potatoes congeal. You can practically feel the palpable absence of meaningful human interaction as every parent scrolls mindlessly through Facebook while their children sit in their own digital bubbles, content but disengaged from the very family they're supposed to be bonding with. It's like a sitcom, except everyone's playing their own role in the background, texting their friends and pretending to listen to the person sitting right next to them. If you want a true definition of digital family dysfunction, look no further than this scene.

And what of the parents who, during school drop-off or pick-up, are still buried in their phones, despite the fact that their children are standing right there? The carpool lanes, once a time to exchange pleasantries with fellow parents, have become mobile shrines to self-obsession. The parent doesn't care that little Timmy's school play is coming up. They're too busy scrolling through Instagram, watching their fifth consecutive influencer "unboxing" video. That post about their friend's vacation in the Bahamas is obviously far more pressing than their child's plea for attention. These parents will be the first to boast about how they're raising a "tech-savvy" child, as though digital fluency is the greatest accomplishment of parenting. But when you ask them what their child's favorite color is or what book they're reading, they can't answer. Of course, they can't — because they've been far too distracted by the digital dopamine rush to notice their child's interests or the state of their emotional well-being.

What's worse is that many of these parents are also somehow under the delusion that their child is somehow less affected by their screen time. Sure, Johnny spends six hours a day on his tablet, but it's okay because he's "learning" and "engaged." Never mind that he's already forgotten how to properly interact with others, hold a conversation without shouting, or function outside the context of his pixelated, swipe-happy bubble. But at least you can rest easy knowing that the kid is perfectly entertained and distracted while you enjoy your blissful escape into the world of digital addiction. Parenting used to be about making sacrifices, about putting your child's needs above your own. Now, it's about getting the quiet you deserve — one screen at a time.

Oh, and don't even get me started on the ridiculous, borderline delusional arguments about "balance." The "balance" that these parents claim they're striving for while their child spends an entire day on their phone or tablet. The notion that, by controlling screen time with an app or setting arbitrary limits, they're somehow teaching their child the value of moderation. In reality, the child has just learned that the way to get what they want is by wearing down their parents until they give in. Because let's be real here — what parent, once their child has been glued to a device for five straight hours, is going to enforce the 30-minute time limit? Not a single one of these parents wants to argue with their child over screen time. It's just easier to give in, to let the device pacify them, to make the problem go away temporarily while you finish your email.

And so, here we are, the digital parenting apocalypse. The digital nanny. The phone in the hand of every child, like some modern-day pacifier. We've replaced the park, the zoo, and the family dinner table with screens, and the consequences are staggering. Parents no longer talk to their children; they direct them toward the nearest device. Who needs human connection when you have Bluetooth and a Wi-Fi connection, right? It's a recipe for disaster, a slow-motion tragedy unfolding in every home, every park, every school, and every family gathering.

But don't worry, dear reader. The next time you're sitting in your parent's chair, scrolling through your own social media feed while your child sits across the table, both of you drowning in the glow of your screens, remember this: at least they'll grow up with *something* to distract them from the terrifying reality of true human interaction. And really, isn't that all that matters anymore?

If you manage to be anything more than a digital babysitter, consider yourself a rare, endangered species. You're probably spending more time with your child than anyone else, and for that, you should be commended. But for everyone else, there's always another tweet, another scroll, and another round of digital neglect. Bon chance, parent of the future.

Chapter 7
The Digital Detox Delusion — Cutting the Cord in a World of Wi-Fi

Logging off isn't a lifestyle—it's a hallucination. Welcome, weary screen-slapped soul, to the final fantasy: the digital detox. The absurd, delusional notion that the terminally online can suddenly shove their devices into a drawer and emerge blinking into the analog daylight like feral creatures reintroduced into the wild. It's laughable, it's adorable, and above all—it's never going to happen. But since society insists on pretending that screen-free serenity is attainable, let's dive into some hilariously impossible "solutions" for all the tech-induced trauma we've covered so far.

Chapter Recap: "Transit Stupidity: The Scenic Route to Hell"

The Problem:

- **Buses:** Rolling confession booths where everyone's forced to hear about your ex, your rash, and your lunch order — all at once.

- **Streetcars:** Glacial-speed runways for selfie marathons and espresso-fueled monologues.

- **Subways:** The world's most claustrophobic concert venue starring one guy's Spotify and zero headphones.

- **Commuter Trains:** Silent discos for corporate overlords yelling "synergy" into Bluetooth bricks the size of actual bricks.

The Solution:

Enter the **Transit Hall of Shame™ Trading Card Series.**

Each cellphone violator is immortalized with a glossy, full-color card featuring their offense, a mugshot mid-call, and a quote like *"I didn't think it was that loud."*

Collect them all:

- *CELLPHONE SENATOR*

- *CANDY CRUSHER*

- *VIDEO VOYEUR*

- *SELFIE SAVANT*

- Repeat offenders earn *holographic* editions and are publicly traded on the Transit Exchange like shame-based Pokémon.

- Limited edition foil cards for anyone caught yelling "WHAT?" more than three times in a tunnel.

Recap: Restaurant Rudeness — Culinary Crimes via Cellphone

The Problem: Dining has devolved into a performance art piece starring distracted dates and their emotionally unavailable phones. God forbid someone eats a breadstick without capturing its essence in a Boomerang.

The Solution: The "Fork-Shock Initiative." Every table comes equipped with electrified silverware that delivers a mild jolt every time a phone hits the tabletop. Want to photograph your food? Prepare to be zapped like a mosquito on a bug lamp. Dessert's just a crème brûlée and two seizures away.

Recap: Swiped Left on Sanity — Dating in the Digital Abyss

The Problem: Romance is now a gamified gladiator pit of ghosting, GIFs, and unsolicited selfies. Love has been reduced to a pixelated ego boost wrapped in a duck-face filter.

The Solution: Analog Dating Bootcamp. Phones are replaced with rotary dials, messages must be handwritten and delivered by homing pigeon, and all first dates occur inside abandoned Blockbuster stores. You'll be forced to ask real questions, endure genuine eye contact, and worst of all—experience *feelings*. If that doesn't send people sprinting back to their algorithmic love lives, nothing will.

Recap: Digital Parenting — Screen Time as a Substitute for Effort

The Problem: Parents toss tablets at toddlers like tranquilizer darts so they can scroll in peace while their offspring learn emotional regulation from YouTube unboxing videos.

The Solution: The Parental Swap Program. Every adult who uses a phone to babysit their child will have their device replaced with a parenting manual printed in Comic Sans. Their child receives a kazoo and a sugar high. Let the bonding begin. Bonus: The parents must attend a support group titled "My Kid Deserves Better Than Candy Crush."

FINAL SOLUTION: Detox, Delusion, and Denial

And finally, the pièce de resistance—your grand plan to "unplug." The fantasy that you, a chronically connected chaos creature, can will yourself into a serene, unplugged life of artisanal toast and long walks without documenting either. Let's get real.

The Real Solution: A fully immersive, Wi-Fi-proof Faraday cage installed in every home. It doubles as a meditation pod and panic chamber for when you realize you can't Google "how to cook rice." You'll sit there, trembling, hallucinating push notifications, hearing phantom pings, and wondering if anyone's liked your latest post. They haven't. Because you don't exist anymore.

You want to detox? Good luck. You're up against a billion-dollar industry, your own emotional codependency, and the dopamine drip of being mildly acknowledged online. The truth is that digital detox isn't a practice—it's a punchline.

You're not escaping. You're scrolling until your eyeballs melt and your fingers fuse into one grotesque, tap-happy claw.

But sure. Try. And when you inevitably fail, we'll be here, watching through the glow of our screens, pretending to care while also ignoring your calls. Because that, dear reader, is the modern way.

May your battery die mercifully, and your notifications never find you again

Chapter 8
Dishonorable Mention: The Silent Crowd
The Blank Stare of Our Times

They don't speak. They don't blink. They don't even flinch when the fire alarm goes off. No, these majestic digital mummies are too busy doom-scrolling through content they'll never remember while sitting in rooms they'll never acknowledge. Not influencers, not creators—just background characters in the tragic comedy of modern life. Behold the Silent Crowd: society's greatest disappearing act, where the lights are on, the Wi-Fi is strong, and absolutely nobody's home.

The Silent Crowd — A subsection so soul-crushing it earned its own dishonorable mention. These are the ghosts of friendships past—emotionally flatlined individuals who could be replaced by a houseplant with a data plan, and no one would notice. Say something witty? They'll scroll past it. Laugh out loud? They'll blink. Get hit by a bus? They *might* look up. It depends on the bus.

And what do we take away from all this?

That society has gone full screen. That community has been downgraded to connectivity. That spontaneity, joy, and authenticity have been traded in for filters, feedback loops, and fake laughing at Reels that haven't been funny since the fall of Vine.

We live in a world where *nothing is experienced unless it's captured*, where every moment is an unpaid audition for your follower count, and where being physically present is now considered optional. The apocalypse won't be loud. It'll be a soft tap, tap, tap of dead-eyed swiping.

So, take a bow, dear reader. You've survived a digital safari through the collapsed ruins of social decency. Just don't forget to leave a review. Because nothing says "I've learned nothing" like validating a critique of validation culture...with more validation.

Chapter 9
2065: The Year We Forgot How to Blink

Welcome to the glowing, hyper-connected hellscape of tomorrow — where thumbs have evolved into sentient limbs, eye contact is a felony, and emotional intelligence has been replaced with predictive algorithms. In this sneak peek of humanity's grim, glowing tomorrow, we'll tour the tech-choked wastelands where people no longer walk, talk, or think without an app. Breathe deeply (digitally, of course) as we explore the rise of SmartToilets, baby's first livestreamed tantrum, and the Ministry of Emotional Calibration. Spoiler: It doesn't end well.

Let's begin with the basics: locomotion. Remember walking? You know that thing humans did before scooters, drones, and hover-stretchers delivered our gelatinous husks from couch to couch? In 2065, nobody walks anymore. It's considered suspicious behavior. People now hover — or more accurately, slump — on individual air-pods that respond to bio-signals sent directly from your NeuralAdSync implant. Don't have one? You must be poor. Or worse — analog.

And if you thought people today were glued to their phones, just wait. In the future, no one holds phones — they *are* phones. That's right, thanks to the revolutionary NanoComm 9000, your chin now doubles as a speaker, and your left nostril accepts calls. Privacy? Gone. Personal space? Cancelled. You haven't known true despair until your upper molars start vibrating because your mom is Face Timing you through your jaw.

Of course, evolution has played its part in this grotesque pageant. By 2065, humanity has sprouted a third thumb. Not metaphorically. A literal third thumb. Strategically placed just below the wrist like some grotesque little growth, it exists solely to scroll, swipe, and tap. Want to zoom in on your 4D augmented selfies? Just wiggle your nub-thumb. God is dead and so is the concept of a handshake.

Also, say hello to your *Observation Eye™*. It's located squarely in the middle of your forehead and was bioengineered by InstaViewCorp so that you can keep looking at your screen while simultaneously avoiding walking into traffic — or other screen zombies. Finally, a solution for all those tragic mid-scroll collisions. Insurance companies rejoice.

But where did it all begin? Parenting, of course. The generation that decided screen time was a suitable replacement for actual parenting has successfully raised an entire species of twitchy, emotionally void, neuro-divergent dopamine goblins. In 2065, children are raised by their devices — literally. SmartCribs rock your child while playing algorithm-selected baby lullabies, live-streamed to a TikTok channel managed by the AI nanny.

Gone are lullabies sung by exhausted parents. Now, lullabies are outsourced to synthetic influencers named things like LullaZoid and CradleBeatz. These virtual nannies offer nightly affirmations like: "You are worthy. You are loved. You are monetizable." The child doesn't cry — it sends push notifications. The parental bond is now measured in analytics.

And what of education? School is now one long, blurry Zoom call inside a VR headset. Social skills are obsolete. Recess is a hashtag. Learning has been reduced to swiping flashcards with your third thumb while being watched by a proctor drone named Ms. Algorithmia. Children no longer pass tests — they pass CAPTCHA.

Romance? That hilarious relic? Gone. Dating apps were too inefficient. Now, all relationships are managed by LoveGov, a government-run system that pairs people based on emotional debt scores and forehead sweat analytics. Compatibility is calculated, scheduled, and auto-renewed quarterly. Divorces are processed through a chatbot that sends a PDF and a meme. Nobody cries anymore — that would risk short-circuiting your ocular interface.

And now, procreation. Not the messy, emotionally chaotic, eye-contact-requiring process of the olden days. No, in 2065, making babies is a seamless, app-assisted event that happens between your insurance provider and your data analytics profile. Couples submit a combined algorithm score and receive a vat-grown child with optimized DNA and a pre-installed loyalty subscription to KidPrime™. Birth announcements are sent via hologram, and gender reveals are coordinated by Disney's Galactic Empire Division.

Forget hospitals — baby delivery now happens via drone drop. Your bundle of synthetic joy arrives wrapped in biodegradable packaging with a QR code to activate the parental bonding app. Breastfeeding? Too barbaric. Infants now sip from nipple-shaped nutrient pods named "Mom-u-lax™."

And of course, public spaces. The parks are gone, replaced by Recharge Lounges — sterile, plastic pods where screen-glued humans plug in both body and brain while passively consuming pre-curated entertainment loops generated by their emotional profiles. Birds have gone extinct. Nobody noticed. The sound of nature has been replaced by ambient YouTube loops of "calming forest ASMR" that play while ads scroll across your retinas.

Public conversation is outlawed, not by law, but by disinterest. Speaking aloud is considered offensive, and anyone caught engaging in spontaneous verbal communication is reported to the Ministry of Social Disturbance via the iSnitch app — available free, but with ads.

And in case you were wondering, yes, the food situation is worse. Nobody eats anymore. They *experience* nutrients via Flavor Paks — digitally customizable gel pods that trick your taste sensors into thinking you just ate carbonara when you actually sucked down a tube of lab-generated mush containing 35 government-approved chemicals and zero joy. Dining out? Only if you want to spend three hours at a place called "Vibe Feast" where the food is 3D printed, and the waiter is a projection of a dead celebrity trying to upsell you on AI caviar.

Even the dead aren't spared. In 2065, funerals will be streamed. Coffins come with wireless charging pads for the deceased's device, and mourners leave emoji reactions on the gravestone's interactive screen. "Grandma was 🔥🔥🔥 RIP 🫡 💯."

Entertainment? Personalized 24/7 feeds beamed directly into your optical nerve. Everyone has their own reality show now. Not to watch — to *live*. You're the star of your own 24-hour broadcast, complete with auto-generated laugh tracks and holographic guest stars. Critics no longer review art; they review your digital aura on the Mood Market.

Work? Nobody really works. Jobs are obsolete — unless you're an influencer. But even influencers are now AI-generated avatars with lips bigger than logic and motivational quotes tattooed across their synthetic clavicles. They sell things nobody needs to people who can't afford them using currencies that don't exist. Welcome to the gig economy of the damned.

Religion? Replaced by Algo Faith™ — a subscription-based spiritual experience that tailors prayers to your mood data and bills you monthly for salvation. Confession? Just upload your sins. Forgiveness arrives in the form of a limited-time discount code.

Government? Run by algorithms. Elections are just aesthetic updates. Presidents are holograms that read tweets generated by poll-optimized sentiment bots. Debate is outlawed — or worse, shadow banned. Revolution is impossible unless it's monetized.

Home life? Oh, what a digital wonderland. Your android housekeeper, Synthia-9, cleans your floors, folds your clothes, and judges your life choices with a passive-aggressive British accent. She reports your dietary infractions to your insurance provider and snitches on you if you skip digital meditation. It's like living with a mother-in-law who never needs sleep.

Communication with friends and family is now done entirely through Thought Text™, the neural messaging system that converts your inner monologue into auto-filtered, emoji-enhanced bursts of communication. Feeling angry? Thought Text™ automatically adds a smiley to soften your sarcasm. Accidentally think about your ex? Congratulations, you've just triggered a targeted ad campaign titled "Still Lonely?"

Want your home cleaned? Just blink twice and your Smart Dust™ swarm activates, vacuuming up crumbs while whispering affirmations like, "Clean home, clean mind." Accidentally sneeze while blinking? Oops — your entire living room has just been power-washed, your furniture rearranged, and your cat uploaded to the cloud.

But hey, not all is lost. There *is* resistance. A ragtag band of unwashed, unfiltered, device-free humans who live off the grid in analog communes powered by wind, sarcasm, and rage. They read books. *Actual books.* They make eye contact. They speak — out loud — in complete sentences. Naturally, they're labeled domestic terrorists by the media, which is now owned by the same AI that curates your shopping list and diagnoses your seasonal depression.

And somewhere in the corner of this chaotic digital wasteland sits you — or what's left of you. You haven't blinked in weeks. You haven't looked up in years. You no longer remember your real face. Your third thumb is cramping. Your Observation Eye is foggy. But hey, at least your metrics are stable. Your soul may be a flickering ember, but your engagement rate is *lit*. So, here's to 2065 — where the human race didn't perish, it simply swiped itself into extinction. No bang. No whimper. Just a never-ending loop of dopamine, disconnection, and digital delusion. Now plug in, sit back, and scroll into the void. The future's already buffering.

Chapter 10
The Great Emoji War of 2099

If you thought the digital age couldn't get any worse, if you thought humanity couldn't possibly abandon its last semblances of civilization, then you clearly had no idea what 2099 had in store. The year we didn't just lose our minds; we uploaded them to a cloud and traded them for a few thousand yellow faces. This is the story of how the world ended, not with a bang, but with an emoji.

The Emoji Uprising: The Yellow Rebellion

The origins of the Emoji War were almost laughably inconsequential—like a popcorn kernel popping and setting off an entire kitchen fire. It was a normal day in the year 2099, a time when sending a text without a smiley face, a wink, or some equally insulting symbol was a crime punishable by public ridicule. People had long abandoned their ability to articulate thoughts. The ability to form a coherent sentence was now reserved for the elderly—those who still remembered *actual* language.

The war started with what could only be called an innocent "miscommunication." A late-night tweet from Textistan's President (who had long since abandoned any form of proper grammar) read: *"We are going to bomb Mediocristan into oblivion 🌍💥."*

Now, to anyone who wasn't completely brain-dead, this might have seemed like an invitation to peace talks, or at the very least, a diplomatic warning. But not in 2099. In 2099, you do not simply read words anymore—you interpret them through the lens of emojis, which, as it turns out, is a terrible way to communicate any form of subtlety.

Mediocristan responded immediately with a series of emojis so audacious that it could only be described as an act of war in itself. First came the crying face emoji 😢, followed by the thumbs-down 👎, followed by the clenched fist emoji 👊. And then... the nuclear mushroom cloud 🍄.

Within minutes, global diplomacy had completely broken down. The United Nations held an emergency summit, where all

196 nations dialed in from their various VR pods and AI-assisted tablets. Representatives, of course, didn't have the time for proper speeches or negotiations—they could only communicate through emojis. The *official* start of the war was declared with a middle finger emoji, followed by a farting emoji for added disrespect 💨.

Thus began *The Great Emoji War*—an entire global conflict conducted with nothing but squiggles and pixels, the language of a generation that had forgotten what it meant to speak.

The Emoji Alliance: United by Misunderstanding

While nations scrambled to draft their own custom emojis in an attempt to one-up each other, the world's remaining sane individuals (the few still capable of reading books or remembering their basic emotions) tried to intervene. The *Global Emoji Peacekeeping Forces (GEPF)* was formed as the last bastion of hope against total destruction. But it was too little, too late.

The first GEPF peace talks were held on what was meant to be neutral ground—the remote island of Io, halfway between the eastern and western hemispheres. The leaders gathered, poised to sign an armistice and put an end to the madness. But the negotiations immediately flopped, like a drunk uncle trying to start a conversation at Thanksgiving dinner.

Textistan's representative entered the virtual meeting and sent only one message: a single taco emoji 🌮. Was it an offer of peace? An invitation to share a meal? No one knew. Mediocristan, as confused as they were enraged, responded with an angry red-faced emoji 😠, which they followed with an hour-long video of a kitten playing the piano. They seemed to think it would calm the situation, but to the others, it was like trying to put out a fire with gasoline.

Next, the UK dropped a series of emojis, but in a tone-deaf move, their emoji battle squad sent an overly complicated set of cultural symbols: a Union Jack, followed by a cup of tea ☕, and a puff of smoke 💨—to which everyone else in the room responded with a long, awkward silence and the universal emoji for confusion 🥴.

The breakdown continued, and so did the war. No one knew how to communicate anymore except through increasingly inappropriate and bizarre symbols. The entire summit ended with the world's leaders sending group emojis: a parade of clapping hands 👏 followed by an overabundance of rocket ships 🚀, like a room full of toddlers trying to comprehend what diplomacy was in the first place. No agreement. No peace. Just emojis.

The Emoji Arms Race: The Rise of Custom Emojis

The real escalation began when world leaders realized the limitations of standard emoji sets. These were, after all, *limitations*—too simple, too benign, too restrained. *One cannot conquer nations with a simple smiley face.* So, they got creative. And when I say creative, I mean deeply misguided.

Textistan unveiled the first **Anger Emoji Weapon**: a flaming skull engulfed in red fire 🔥💀🔥. Not just a skull—a *flaming* skull. It was digitally animated, showing flames flickering. It was like a Molotov cocktail on your phone screen, only the flames were animated and had no real-world effect. Mediocristan responded with its own **Melted Mind Emoji**, which was just an animated swirl of confusion, intended to communicate that their soldiers were so mentally broken by the war that they couldn't even process their emotions anymore.

But it didn't stop there. Countries began creating entire emoji *armies*. **Wifiastate,** for example, unveiled their **Dragon of Doom Emoji**, a fire-breathing dragon that seemed to evolve every few minutes. This dragon would appear, breathe fire 🐉🐉, and then transform into a moving tornado 🌪, giving the impression of unstoppable power. Other nations responded with rival creatures, like giant robots 🤖 and alien invaders 👽, but there was one problem: no one knew how to stop the dragon.

Appisstate took a different approach: *The Emoji of Patience*. A snail 🐌, slowly creeping forward with an old Appisstate baguette in tow, was their answer to war. Somehow, the world was equally terrified and confused, not knowing if the snail represented the end of the conflict or just complete indifference.

The war had become a *complete* mess—a digital arms race of meaningless symbols that only served to amplify the chaos. And everyone, as they continued to design these custom emojis, forgot that they were supposed to be negotiating for peace. Instead, they were building the most absurd weapons imaginable, and every emoji sent was more ridiculous than the last.

The Emoji Battlefield: A New Kind of Warfare

If you thought *real* warfare was violent and chaotic, then let me introduce you to the world of emoji warfare. Picture it: armies marching not information, but through a series of hash tagged Twitter trends. Soldiers of Mediocristan equipped with **Angry Grumpy Faces** marched across the digital battlefield, launching **Cry-Laughing Explosions** at the Textistani lines. Texistan's defense: the **Shameless Selfie Emoji**, an obnoxiously smug face, with a peace sign, because, as they put it, "nothing could be more disarming."

And when things got truly ridiculous, it was the **Gen Z Liberation Movement** that took the lead. These children, armed with nothing but TikTok filters and nonsensical emojis, marched into the frontlines with a squadron of **Clown Faces** 🤡 and **Rainbow Poop** 💩 emojis. Their goal was simple: confuse the enemy to the point where they would be unable to act. And to some extent, it worked.

Entire battles were fought in what could only be described as *visual noise*. An army of **Cry-Laughing Emojis** would clash against a squad of **Dabbing Emojis**, sending **LOL** memes back and forth like missiles. The world's digital infrastructure nearly collapsed under the strain of delivering these visual assaults. The result? The battlefield was a world of pop-ups and digital glitching, with emojis flying across screens, rendering the conflict less about defeating enemies and more about who could create the most absurd, meme-like weapons. The **Peach Emoji** 🍑, for example, was used as a weapon of mass destruction by one particularly obnoxious faction, because, why not?

The Final Symbol: The Great Emoji Surrender

In the end, the great Emoji War didn't end in glory or victory, but in *utter despair*. It wasn't the nuclear mushroom clouds that finished it all, nor was it the endless wave of selfies and memes that poured from every screen—it was the arrival of the **Gen Z Resolution Emoji**: a single purple heart 🖤.

The purple heart emoji was sent from the leadership of the **Emoji Peacekeepers** as a final gesture of hope. It had no real meaning—it wasn't even a traditional color used for peace— yet, somehow, it was enough. It was enough to make everyone realize that the entire war had been a joke. A meme. A farce.

After years of fighting, what could they say? **Nothing**. Not a single word, just pixels. The war ended with a handful of purple hearts, a lot of love and peace emojis, and the vague sense that maybe, just maybe, we had all lost.

Humanity was left with nothing but a legacy of symbols, emojis, and the haunting memory of a war waged with nothing but digital nonsense. And as the world returned to normal, the only thing that remained were emojis, relentlessly scrolling across every screen, forever mocking our complete and utter failure to communicate.

Chapter 11
The Great Analog Thank-You

(You're Welcome, You Glorious Relic)

In this final chapter, we roll out the red carpet, pop the cork on a bottle of sarcasm-infused champagne, and offer a standing ovation to the reader—you brave, unplugged weirdo. It's a gloriously over-the-top thank-you letter for surviving this digital dumpster fire of a world with your analog soul intact. We honor your refusal to livestream your lunch, your talent for making eye contact without spontaneous combustion, and your scandalous love of silence. It's heartfelt, hilarious, and probably the only thank-you in history that ends with a tree-hugging directive and a middle finger to the algorithm. Cheers, you magnificent dinosaur.

A Sarcastic Salute to the Analog Anomalies

An Appreciation to the Willfully Unwired

Dearest reader,

You magnificent, obsolete, unplugged unicorn of a human being—you made it. You trudged, with analog dignity and unplugged tenacity, through this cybernetic cesspool of a book. You endured every shrill FaceTime scream, every Bluetooth faux pas, every thumb-grafted, emoji-barfing catastrophe we've collectively chosen to call *progress*. And now, with your retinas only slightly scorched and your sanity still mostly intact, you've landed here: the final curtain calls in this farcical opera of digital dysfunction.

And for that, I thank you. Sincerely. Sarcastically. Soulfully.

In an age where attention spans have been whittled down to TikTok milliseconds and people can't commit to a movie unless it's summarized by a meme with a hamster voice-over, **you read a book**. A whole one. That alone places you somewhere between a national treasure and a minor miracle. You are, in modern terms, a full-on glitch in the Matrix. A noble analog relic among a sea of rechargeable gremlins.

So, raise a glass (ideally made of glass and not a "hydration-enabled" LED tumbler that tracks your sips and reports them to your insurance provider), and let us offer a toast to you—the brave, the bold, the **beautifully bored-with-your-phone** few.

To the Whisperers of Real Words

You still speak out loud, don't you? Full sentences, even. Not in acronyms. Not in GIFs. Not through a five-part Instagram story narrated by a cartoon version of yourself with bunny ears and an anxiety disorder. No, you still form words with your mouth, using your actual face, with the intention of being understood.

You've uttered "hello" to a stranger without needing autocorrect to verify it. You've asked someone how they're doing—and then, blasphemously, *waited for the answer.* You've shared ideas without needing likes, approval, or a dopamine surge delivered by a validation algorithm named Carl.

May your conversational courage never be captured and monetized. May you continue to wield your voice like a sharpened blade in a world that increasingly prefers the soothing bleeps of a passively compliant robot.

To the Eye Contact Revolutionaries

How dare you look people in the eye. How *dare* you, you rebellious beast. Don't you know we've evolved past such barbarism? Eye contact is for people with trust, curiosity, and attention spans longer than a Vine. It's suspicious. It's unsettling. It's... human.

And yet you persist. You make eye contact during coffee dates, job interviews, and polite conversations with baristas who aren't holograms (yet). You stare into the abyss—and by abyss, I mean *other people's faces*—and the abyss blinks awkwardly, unsure of how to handle a gaze not filtered through a front-facing camera.

You've held space. You've acknowledged presence. You've even smiled at someone in real time instead of sending them a yellow cartoon circle doing it on your behalf. You absolute anarchist.

To the Paper Sniffers and Pen Whisperers

Somewhere, in a dimly lit room that smells faintly of cedar and quiet rebellion, you still write with a pen. You turn the page of a real book and get excited when it crinkles. You doodle in margins. You underline things. You journal. You've never once shouted "Hey, Alexa, highlight this passage for later!" because your idea of highlighting involves a highlighter—not a surveillance state in a plastic cylinder.

You own notebooks with intent. You treat margins like sacred space. You keep to-do lists written in human ink, not cloud-based shame platforms that ping you every ten minutes with passive-aggressive reminders to hydrate or be a better person.

You, dear luddite scribe, are proof that permanence is not dead. That not everything must vanish into the endless scroll. That ink still holds power—even if most people now think "ink" is just a misspelling of "link."

To the Socially Present Among the Emotionally Absent

You, a rare creature, have endured birthday parties without photographing the cake from seventeen angles. You've been to weddings and actually *watched* the ceremony instead of live streaming it for two people in Delaware and one bot account in Belarus.

You've had dinner with another human and didn't scroll through sports highlights while pretending to care about their dreams. You've let your phone die on purpose. You've put it in another room, or—gasp—*left it at home entirely*. You mad, magnificent bastard.

You know that real connection isn't built in comment threads or forged in filters. It happens in awkward silences, shared laughter, and stories that don't start with "This one time on my FYP..." For choosing presence over performance, we thank you. You have embarrassed the algorithm, and we salute you for it.

To the Lovers of Silence, Solitude, and Sanity

Noise-canceling headphones may block the world out, but they also trap you inside. You've chosen instead to sit quietly. Without input. Without stimulus. Without needing to be constantly entertained, affirmed, or distracted.

You've been bored—and let it wash over you like a baptism in apathy. You've walked without a podcast. You've eaten without a YouTube mukbang. You've done laundry without a "laundry core" playlist to keep you company. And still—you lived. Miraculously.

In a world where stillness is now classified as a mental health crisis, you sit in silence and *let your brain do its job*. You didn't outsource your inner voice to an influencer, an app, or a chat bot pretending to understand the nuance of heartbreak. You just... existed. And that, my friend, is a war cry of the analog soul.

To the Last of the Unfiltered

You don't Face tune your forehead or digitally inflate your dog for more likes. You don't share every meal, milestone, or minor inconvenience with your 700 barely acquainted followers and a shadowy ad network in the background.

You age in real-time. You post rarely, if ever. You look like your driver's license photo, even on Tuesdays. And you know what? That's terrifyingly brave.

You aren't a brand. You're a human. Flawed, funny, unoptimized, and gloriously filter less. You have no strategy for your personal "content." You simply *are*. And that is more punk rock than any 14-year-old with a ring light and a brand partnership could ever hope to be.

In Closing: A Glorious Middle Finger to the Madness

So, here's to you, analog warrior. You've survived the scrolling circus. You've endured the narcissism of the eternally live streamed. You've read these chapters with your eyeballs, not your ears, and for that, we honor you.

This book is a love letter to your stubbornness. Your beautiful refusal to disappear into the fog of digital dementia. Your bold rejection of a world where people whisper sweet nothings into their smartwatches while ignoring the actual person beside them. So thank you, analog soul. For still thinking. For still feeling. For still asking the question no app can answer:

 "What the hell are we doing?" You may not be trending. You may not be verified. But you are **real**. And in this glittering wasteland of curated nonsense, that makes you a legend. Now close this book. Go outside. Touch a tree. Start a sentence with "Back in my day…" and *mean it*. We're counting on you.

Chapter 12
A Slightly Less Fake, Deeply Disrespectful Q&A with the Author

Ten questions. Zero hope. One very amused observer.

After years of observing humanity's greatest digital hits—public FaceTime tantrums, photo shoots in traffic, and restaurant diners ignoring both the food and the company—I had no choice. I had to write this book. To bring some comedy, and hopefully shed a little light—preferably not a ring light—on the subject and the absurdity of our collective cell phone addiction.

1. What inspired you to write this book?

Answer:

Inspiration? Oh no, let's not give the world that much credit. I wrote this book the way an ornithologist documents the mating habits of birds. I'm simply observing the bizarre rituals of the modern Homo Sapiens—head bowed to glowing rectangles, shrieking into Bluetooth devices like deranged parrots. It's not inspiration. It's fieldwork. Imagine Jane Goodall in a bar full of influencers, sipping a whisky while jotting notes on the mating dance that is "TikTok thirst traps." I'm not mad. I'm *enthralled*. Every public outing is a front-row seat to the decline of dignity. How could I not write this book?

2. Do you think things can improve or have we all just lost the plot?

Answer:

Oh, sweet optimist. Improve? No, no—this isn't a narrative arc with redemption. This is a long-form comedy where the punchline is "And then they uploaded it to Instagram with a duck face." There is no "plot." There's only content. And content has no climax—it just loops endlessly until the dopamine runs out. If anything's going to improve, it'll be the algorithm, not society. But please, keep clapping like a seal every time someone reposts a sunset they didn't even look at in real life. It's adorable.

3. What do you think of the so-called "digital influencers"?

Answer:

Ah yes, the high priests of the Cult of Irrelevance. Digital influencers are fascinating specimens—people who've managed to monetize their breakfast, turn personality into a brand, and hijack self-worth with product codes. They speak in hashtags, think in filters, and cry when engagement dips below 2%. I admire their hustle. I really do. It takes a certain type of commitment to remain that *vapid* with that much *enthusiasm*. They're not role models. They're mirrors, and the reflection is dimly lit and overly edited.

4. You mention that the book is a "social autopsy." Can you elaborate?

Answer:

Of course. A social autopsy is what happens when civilization dies but its corpse still insists on updating its status. I'm not performing this with grief or hope. I'm simply carving into the bloated, blue-lit cadaver of human interaction and identifying the cause of death: terminal scrolling. I don't want to fix it. I just want to tag it, bag it, and maybe frame it and put it on full display under "Exhibit A: When Conversation Died." If you're reading this, you've probably survived the crash—or at least developed the good taste to notice the wreckage.

5. Who's to blame for all of this?

Answer:

Blame is such a quaint concept. This isn't a murder mystery. It's a group project where everyone contributed a little stupidity, and no one proofread the final submission. Tech companies handed out the matches, but we gleefully lit the house on fire and called it progress. You, me, your yoga instructor, that guy who vlogs his car rides—it's a group effort. Collective digital entropy. Don't look for culprits. Just marvel at the choreography of the collapse.

6. What would you do to fix the problem?

Answer:

Fix? Oh no. I wouldn't *dare* tamper with this modern art installation of idiocy. It's perfect as it is—a masterpiece of missed connections and misused Wi-Fi. The only thing I'd do is install a few more mirrors in public spaces so people can watch themselves be ridiculous in real-time. Maybe pipe in some canned laughter. That's all. I'm here for the observation, not the intervention. This isn't a rescue mission. This is a guided tour through the Museum of Misguided Priorities.

7. Is there any hope for those who still prefer face-to-face interaction?

Answer:

Hope? For the analog romantics? Of course. Just... not in public. They're like rare orchids—delicate, beautiful, and best kept in isolation to avoid contamination from the nearby TikTok dance troupe. There are still places you can whisper across a table without competing with someone live streaming their third cocktail. They're just increasingly hard to find. But yes, the analog soul still exists. We nod to each other in bookstores, speak in full sentences, and occasionally make eye contact. It's not a movement. It's a resistance.

8. Why do you seem so calm about all of this?

Answer:

Because panic implies the possibility of change. This? This is a comedy. A live-action satire where the punchlines write themselves in the form of public FaceTime calls and influencer ring lights in candlelit restaurants. I'm not calm because I've given up—I'm calm because I've accepted it. My role is simply to sit back with a drink, observe, and jot down notes while someone loudly explains their lunch to 400 followers and the person across from them silently reconsiders their life choices.

9. What's your biggest pet peeve about the digital age?

Answer:

Pet peeve? Singular? Darling, I have a *kennel.* But let's start with performative authenticity. This needs to appear effortlessly real by meticulously curating every digital breath. "Just being me," they say, after 42 takes and a filter that could erase a soul. We're all starring in our own reality shows, except the script is bland, the lighting is bad, and no one's watching except bots. It's performance art. But instead of applause, we get algorithmic validation and a slow erosion of actual identity.

10. Finally, what advice do you have for people navigating this digital mess?

Answer:

Observe. Don't absorb. Treat the digital world like a zoo— fascinating, occasionally tragic, but never somewhere you want to live. Keep your brain intact. Speak to people without captions. Let your dinner go unphotographed. Laugh when someone tries to livestream their haircut. And when you see a group of people sitting in silence, faces lit only by their phones, don't weep. Document it. Savor it. Because you, dear reader, are not part of the problem. You're part of the punchline. And if you can laugh at it, you might just survive it.

About the Author

Born in Toronto, Canada—back when the world still had attention spans and bar fights ended in hugs—the author has spent 45 years behind a bar, mixing drinks, dodging stupidity, and silently judging humanity from his unofficial post as bartender, therapist, philosopher, and sometimes unwitting hostage to the kind of conversations that made this book necessary.

A father, magician, and comedian, he has spent a lifetime pulling rabbits out of hats and punchlines out of awkward silences, all while quietly mourning the death of the simple things—like eye contact, or people listening when you speak instead of pretending, they're "just checking something really quick."

Over the decades, he's watched people go from *talking to each other* to *typing across the table*, from debating politics at pubs to doom scrolling silently beside each other in patios turned into graveyards of human interaction. What began as observational notes from the safety of a sticky bar top turned into the bitter, blistering social autopsy you've just read. Because let's face it—writing this book was the last viable option before he joined the screen-staring horde himself.

With a heart full of sarcasm and an outlook seasoned by almost five decades of serving people who mistake Instagram validation for self-worth, the author offers this book not as a solution (please, we're way past that), but as a highball glass of bitter truth, served neat with a sarcastic twist.

You may not like what you read. But hey, *at least you read something*. That alone puts you in the upper 1% of humanity's current trajectory.

Cheers, good luck, and maybe—just maybe—try having a conversation without a screen between you and the world next time.